Gre

Night Hov

Marissa Ann

Table of Contents

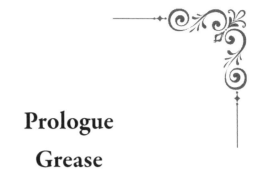

Prologue
Grease

Watching my President of the club get married earlier to the woman he loves actually puts a smile on my face. Something that rarely happens these days.

I figure my marrying days have long since passed since I am turning forty-two this year. I am always too busy with work and helping to change the club over to more legal activities.

No one would want an old fucker like me anyways. I can't even imagine having kids now. Hell, I would be almost sixty before they got grown.

However, that doesn't mean that I don't still love a good romp in the sheets with a beautiful woman.

Walking around the reception at the clubhouse, I've spotted the one I want to hear screaming my name later.

She's fucking gorgeous in that simple way women sometimes have. I don't think she's even wearing makeup which in my opinion is a good thing.

Most these women gob that shit on like a mask, so when you wake up next to them in the morning light you are asking yourself what the fuck you were thinking.

She has long gorgeous red hair that shines in the sunlight. She must have come straight here from work, as she's wearing scrubs with a name tag.

She's currently talking to Jade who is standing next to Reaper, so I can use his ass as an excuse to get closer and at least find out her name.

As I walk up, it sounds like they are talking about Cole so this chick must work at the clinic where Jade takes the kids for check-ups.

Her eyes look over at me and then away before returning again.

I give her my best smile as I look her up and down until Reaper elbows me in the ribs.

"Don't worry Britni, he may look intimidating but he's just a big teddy bear." Jade says while looking at me with slitted eyes.

"Name's Grease." I hold my hand out to her in which she takes it.

Her hands are soft just as I knew they would be from working in a doctor's office.

"Britni. It's nice to meet you." She introduces herself before pulling her hand away again.

I'm a little surprised to realize I miss the feeling of it in my own.

Britni

Coming to Jade's wedding and reception, I wasn't sure what to expect.

We have all heard the rumors that circle around the Night Howler's club but I had promised I would be here as soon as I could get off work.

Jade and I became friends after she started bringing the kids into the clinic where I work. She's such a great mom to her kids so I figured the club couldn't be that bad.

Everything was beautiful during the wedding and all the guys were very respectful towards me. It wasn't until I met Grease that I felt uncomfortable.

He looked at me as if he could already see my naked body underneath my scrubs.

The feeling of his rough hand in my own when we met, sent chill bumps down my body causing my nipples to tingle.

He might be a little older than me but the man was hot as sin with eyes that made it even more scorching hot outside.

Even after talking to Jade while he just stood there staring at me, I could still feel his eyes on me as I walked around talking to the others.

I'm standing at the table to get a drink when I feel a body push into me from behind. I seem to already know who it is.

"Just grabbing a beer darling." He murmurs next to my ear, reaching across the table to grab a cold one from the iced down tub.

Not saying a word, I turn my head to look directly into his eyes. My breathing picks up and my body stands to attention as it notices the hardness of his pressing even more into me from behind.

Feeling bold. I press back into him with a small smile, lifting my eyebrow.

"How about we go somewhere a little quieter so that I can hear every sigh that escapes that beautiful mouth before you scream my name." He whispers, running his tongue along the shell of my ear.

"Yes." Is all I breathe out before he grabs my hand and pulls me with him across the yard stopping next to a huge bike.

Holding out a helmet, he waits to see if I take it before climbing on.

"Have you ever ridden before?" He asks.

"Not a bike." I state with a smile that makes him grin.

"Just climb on, put your feet on the pegs there and hold on tight." He grins back.

I put the helmet on and climb on, wrapping my arms around his waist. In just a few more minutes, we are flying down the road and I am loving every second of it.

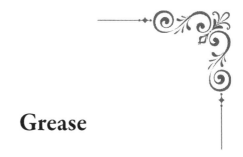

Grease

Two nights later, we're both lying in my big bed in a tangle of sweaty limbs with her red hair splayed across the pillow she's laying on.

"Well that was fun." She says into the darkness and I chuckle at her assessment.

"Extremely but if you'll give me a few more minutes I'll make you scream my name again." I rub my slick cock against her soaking wet pussy gaining a gasp for my efforts.

"You are insatiable." She laughs, pushing on my shoulder.

"I think it's the hair." I whisper, running one hand through the softness around her face.

"I should probably go." She whispers a few minutes later.

For some reason my heart kicks up at the thought of her walking away right now. I've not had my fill of her body just yet or her company.

The woman is funny. Quirky even in an adorable kind of way and I find myself wanting to be around her some more just to hear the things she might say.

"We're leaving for a rally down South in the morning. Come with me. You'd like it and we could have a few more days of fun." I blurt out, surprising even myself.

While I may be tired of the one night stands with women it's very unlike me to commit to more than one night with them in a row.

Most women nag too fucking much to want to be around them for a prolonged period of time.

"It's a little soon for that, don't you think?" She laughs. "Besides, I believe we both agreed that this was only a weekend fling."

"We can go as friends. No strings." I shrug. "You'll have fun. Most everyone from the wedding will be there so you'll certainly not lack for people to hang out with. A bike I've been working on for over a year is being unveiled there on Saturday."

For the life of me, I have no idea why I'm pushing her so hard to go with me to the rally. There's always plenty of pussy there a man can sink his cock into if he wants it.

Something inside of me though isn't wanting to let go of this woman just yet.

Being someone who believes in spirituality a little differently than others, I've learned to listen to that small voice inside of me when it comes to these kinds of things.

Nothing in life is by chance. There's normally a reason behind everything including our paths crossing at the wedding of one of my brothers from the club.

"I am due for a vacation and it does sound like fun." She says after a few minutes.

"So you want to go?" I ask, holding my breath waiting for her to answer.

She laughs, shaking her head. "Why not."

"Fuck yes!" I roll her over, pinning her under me. "Now where was I?" I whisper against her lips as my cock springs back to life and I slide back inside of her.

Damn she feels good.

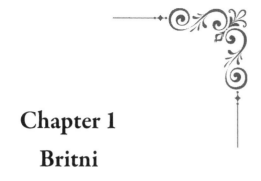

Chapter 1
Britni

I don't know what came over me to agree to coming here. It's as if I completely lost my mind. I, more than anyone, know what's at stake.

Three years ago I ran away from one of the most brutal motorcycle clubs on the FBI's radar.

For over a year, I was kept basically as a prisoner by them until an undercover agent helped me to escape.

After changing my name and relocating to North Mississippi, everything has been quiet.

I hear from the agent about once a year when he checks in with me. Last I spoke to him six months ago, they still haven't collected enough evidence to put the whole club behind bars. Not even with the limited information that I was able to give.

The only thing that made everything a little easier for me was that I had no family that would miss me.

Just a few friends. One of which, I was told, filed a missing person's report on me a few weeks after I went missing.

The agent made sure the report got buried so that I could fully disappear without any issues. After they moved me here,

I found out about the Night Howler's being in the area and I stayed clear of anyone wearing a club emblem.

Until Jade came along with her sweet friendly face and two amazing children. She and I became friends pretty quickly.

It wasn't until later that I learned that she was involved with Reaper, the President of the Night Howler's.

She even brought him along to several of the appointments. He was always nice and extremely respectful even when Jade wasn't around. I figured with a President like him, his club couldn't be all that bad.

By the night of the wedding, I had been around several of the club members on more than one occasion. Each time, they were all nice, respectful men who loved to play with the kids and laugh at their antics.

Grease was a new face in the crowd that night and I noticed him immediately. He was definitely what we call a silver fox if ever I'd seen one.

Although older, he was built to perfection with muscled arms that clearly stated he'd have no issues tossing me around in the bedroom.

I've been careful since moving to Mississippi to not get attached to anyone. Not that I've gone without the occasional company of a man but some of them have felt like duds between the sheets.

I've always been up front with them all that we would never go further than the night or two that I spent with them although several have still tried.

Why is it that it's perfectly okay when a man does it but when a woman does it, people want to act like she committed the ultimate sin?

"Hey. You coming?" Grease sticks his head into our camper with a huge grin.

"Yeah. I'll be right there." I smile back as he closes the door behind him.

Going into the bathroom, I check my makeup in the mirror as well as my hair.

I'm still not used to the red color and it's a pain in the ass to have it touched up every couple of weeks.

I'm naturally a light brunette with red highlights but when I changed my name I also had to change the way I looked.

Here, in this place, surrounded by bikers, I'm even more thankful to have changed my appearance. I don't believe that the Demon Riders would be here but there's always a chance.

I plan to stay as close to Grease as I can possibly get and hope like hell no one recognizes me.

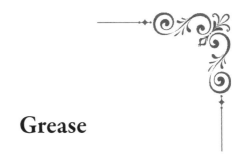

Grease

"**F**ucking hell, there's a lot of people here this year." Reaper looks around at the crowds of people milling about. "Loki, make sure all the guys know to keep a close eye on any of our girls. I'd hate to have to start a war with another club for touching what belongs to us."

Loki nods and walks off to spread the word. While the women with us typically are marked by wearing jackets that proclaim them as taken, men who've been drinking sometimes forget to look past a pair of tits to realize the woman would not be willing.

"You make sure Britni has her jacket on at all times. Jade told me she loaned her one. I'll get everyone rounded up and we'll see you at the stage." He tells me before moving off to find the others.

Looking back at my camper, I sigh, wondering if I need to go poke my head in there again to get her to come on before we are late. I'm about to head that way when I feel a soft hand on my arm.

"Grease! I'm so glad you came again this year."

Glancing down at the woman, she looks vaguely familiar but I'd hate to be rude and flat ask her if I know her.

13

"Of course I came this year. A bike I built is in the contest." I step back slightly to remove her hand from my arm but she just steps forward, following me and pushing her tits even closer.

"I bet it's big and strong just like you. Maybe we can go watch the show together, then we can have a little bit of fun like last year. It broke my heart when you just left without a goodbye." She pokes her lip out, then pulls it between her teeth.

I assume she's trying for a look of sexiness but it's nowhere near sexy. Fucking hell, have I had sex with this woman?

"Or if you like, I can give you a little something right now to tide you over until later. Hmm?" She pushes even closer.

I'm about to shove her away when I hear a giggle behind me and I know it to be Britni. I'm a little disappointed by the sound. Even though we've not been around each other enough for her to be jealous, it stings a little that she isn't at least somewhat territorial instead of giggling at the situation.

"Hey baby. You ready?" I extricate myself from the woman and grab Britni, pulling her under my arm.

She allows me to do so, not even saying anything about my term of endearment but her grin doesn't fade.

"You're attached?" The other woman stomps a little and huffs away.

"Well that was entertaining." Britni giggles again, staring at the woman's retreating back.

"I'm so glad you're having fun at my expense." I droll.

"Who was she anyway?" She asks curiously.

"Would you think less of me if I said that I had no idea?" I look down into her eyes that never waiver.

"Nope. But I'll not let you forget that a woman you have obviously had sex with, came onto you and you looked terrified."

"Terrified? I didn't look terrified." I protest as we begin making our way through the crowds.

"You actually did. I just don't know if it's because you couldn't remember her or because you were afraid of how I'd react."

"Maybe a little of both." I answer honestly but don't look at her. Scanning the crowd I find my brothers close to the stage and head in their direction.

"There you two are. I was beginning to wonder if you got lost." Jade smiles, pulling Britni into the middle with the rest of the girls from our club.

Standing there with my brothers, we listen to the announcer welcoming everyone to the rally. As he goes into the details of the bikes that are going to be on display, I watch Britni out of the corner of my eye.

Since we arrived yesterday, this is probably only the second time I've been able to get her to leave the camper. Once last night, she distracted me by getting fully naked. Watching her now, questions are beginning to raise inside my head.

She isn't listening to the announcer or looking at the stage at all. Instead, she's scanning the faces in the crowd.

A bike rally just doesn't seem like her kind of scene, so who could she possibly be looking for here in this huge crowd of bikers?

When she notices me watching her, she smiles, turning her attention to Jade's sister, Fire, who's currently sneaking up behind Spark with a water bottle.

Spark goes stiff as a board when the cold water hits his head. Once the bottle is completely empty, Fire begins to back away slowly while laughing hysterically. As he turns her way, he says with deadly calm, "Run."

Not needing to be told a second time, she takes off through the crowd with Spark in hot pursuit leaving behind the rest of us laughing at their antics.

The two of them still haven't worked out their problems since Jade finally came back home where she belongs. I'm not sure if they ever will.

Those two were always best friends growing up. To me, that would be the perfect relationship. To be best friends first then turn into something more.

I think for Fire it did turn into something more but Spark, the stubborn ass that he is just hasn't realized it yet.

He was even stupid enough to hand her divorce papers a while back with a smile. The rest of us saw what was coming but he apparently didn't.

By the time she was done, Spark had a black eye and a few blisters on his hands from trying to put out the fire that she set using the divorce papers.

He then wondered obliviously for two weeks as to why the hell she stopped talking to him.

"You ever going to talk to that knuckle headed brother of yours about his marriage?" I ask Reaper.

"Hell no. That's their business. Besides, he'll either figure it out or Fire will kill him first." He grins back at me as he turns towards his wife.

I can't stop the smile on my face from watching these two. They had so many problems but they worked it out and are happier than I've ever seen them.

I want that. Someone that makes me so completely happy that others can't stop themselves from smiling at us.

Maybe I'm going through a midlife crisis or some shit. Ten years ago it didn't bother me that I hadn't found someone to spend the rest of my life with or that I hadn't had any kids.

These days though, I wonder more often if I missed out on something great by not having any little ones. I've truly enjoyed playing with the kids in the club. The Prez's kids are amazing and I don't mind when they want me to give them "horsey rides" on the floor.

Is it really too late for me to at least have someone in my life that I can be happy with?

Looking back over at Britni, she looks back at me with a tiny grin before walking straight to my side and putting my arm around her.

"Your bike's next!" She says excitedly, watching the stage but my eyes stay on her.

She's fucking beautiful as hell and for some reason, I've loved every second that we've spent together instead of getting bored with her company.

If I can have this for the next week, I think I'd die a happy enough man.

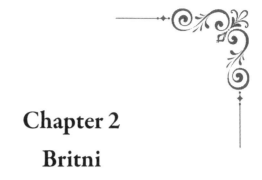

Chapter 2
Britni

I'm just stepping into the shower after yet another sweaty round with Grease when he opens the door and walks in naked.

"What do you think you're doing?" I ask seriously.

"I figured we could save time by getting in the shower together." He wiggles his brows and I can't stop the smile I give him.

"Save time, huh? Think you can keep your hands to yourself long enough to save time?" I laugh as he steps in behind me.

Grabbing me around the waist, pulling my back to his front, he whispers into my ear, "Nope." He pushes his now hard as a rock erection against my ass and I can't stop the groan that escapes my lips.

Putting my hands up on the shower wall, I lean forward, pushing myself even harder back into him.

He moves slightly so that his cock glides between my slick folds between my legs, rubbing against my most sensitive nub.

He knows exactly how to play my body like the finest instrument.

His hands slide up my back, massaging as he goes, sliding back down to rub down my ass and thighs all while he moves back and forth hitting my clit just right with the tip of his cock.

It's the best torture I've ever experienced in my life. It's never been this good with anyone in all the years that I've been old enough to even notice men.

"You ready for me baby?" He asks, leaning forward to kiss along the back of my neck as his hands take my breasts, kneading them gently.

"God, yes." I manage to say, hoping he'll slam into my throbbing center.

"Are you sure?" He asks with a chuckle as I'm pushing back onto him trying to seat myself and take what I want.

"I swear to God! Stop torturing me!" I growl. My hands are curled into fists, my body throbbing all over and my nipples tingling with anticipation.

He slides back and forth several more long minutes as I pant in front of him.

I've been with him long enough now even though it's been only a week, to know that the man will only give me what I want in instances like this when he's good and damn ready to.

When I finally feel him at my entrance, I hold myself back from pushing down onto his cock as I know he'll start his torture all over again.

While it all seems to build us both up to the most explosive orgasms ever, we are already late for lunch with the others.

He pushes in slowly, my body wound so tight it already feels like I'm about to explode but he doesn't move immediately.

"Fuck! I love the way your ass fits against me so well." He growls and I feel his cock throb deep inside of me.

As he begins to move, he takes no time to build up in rhythm, preferring instead to slam back inside of me quickly hitting that perfect spot just right.

I'm screaming through my orgasm within moments, my insides squeezing him tightly as he follows me over that edge into bliss a few minutes later.

Laying my head onto the shower wall, it's a cool contrast to the heat of the water cascading down on us both.

Pulling himself free of me, he spins me around, holding me against the wall as his mouth takes my own. The slickness of his cock grounding into my stomach.

Breaking the kiss, we're both breathing hard, staring back at each other.

"I think I'll just keep you forever." He grins.

"Think you can handle me forever?" I tease back.

"Sure I do. Give me lip and I'll just fuck you until you can't talk. It seems to work for the Prez with his woman." He laughs, pulling back and grabbing the soap.

"Better not let Jade hear you say such things. Reaper may wind up sleeping outside."

"Have I told you about the time that Fire actually burned down the cabin he was holed up in back when Jade ran off years ago?" He asks and I look at him like he's lost his mind.

"You can't be serious."

"As a heart attack! She was so pissed at him that she found where he was staying, found him passed out naked inside and set the fucker on fire."

"You're making that up. I can believe an accident maybe but not that." I laugh, shaking my head.

"Ask Jade if you don't believe me. She knows all about it. The women in this club are more ruthless than us men." He says with a seriousness that I almost believe him.

"I can't believe a guy like Reaper would allow her to get away with such a thing." I look at him with a raised brow.

While I've seen them all be respectful, I know what kind of men are in a motorcycle club. The ruthlessness is just under the surface. It could take the smallest thing for it to come out and all hell would break loose.

Even this fine ass man standing in front of me. I don't seriously trust completely that he'd not turn on me in a second.

"Men aren't that nice." I say out loud accidentally and he spins back in my direction.

"What's that supposed to mean?" He asks.

The hair on my arms begins to raise as my heart beats faster in my chest.

"I didn't mean to offend you." I say quickly, taking a step back from him.

His brows draw together as he regards me and I wait to see if this is the exact explosion I was just talking about in my head.

"You done in this shower? You're getting all wrinkly." He grins, pulling the door open and stepping out of the shower leaving me a bit more confused about this man I can't seem to get enough of.

I've not had many good experiences when it comes to men. I've had a few that were nice enough. Some I even slept with even if I did have to get myself off later after having to fake an orgasm.

I'm still asking myself what in the hell about him made me get on that bike that night and why the hell I'm still at his side a week later.

He's handsome and sweet at times but how long could that possibly last? And do I seriously want to have to run for my life from yet another club?

While I have a hard time believing in how nice all of these people are in the Night Howler's, I feel myself wanting to believe it.

I see how their women look at them. Not with fear but with love. Even when they play jokes on each other, there's never any fear in their eyes.

I find myself wanting that. Longing for it. I'm tired of being alone. I want to love and be loved. But can I have that with a man in a club that may or may not get up to all kinds of things? Maybe even murder.

Too many questions but it's way too early in our one week together to even be thinking about the long term.

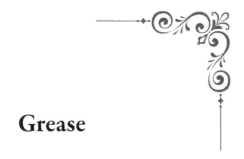

Grease

"I can't believe they are here this year." Reaper says with a slight nod towards two Demon Rider's as they drive by.

"Me either. They fuckers need to all be in shallow graves South of fucking the border." Growls Skeeter, the Prez of one of our sister clubs down in New Orleans.

"I noticed that one on the left was staring at our group of women during the revealing of the bikes." Reaper says, surprising me as I never noticed. Only thing I noticed during the reveal was Britni.

"I'd say keep them close but I'm sure you've already thought of that." He says.

We all watch as the assholes get swallowed up by the crowd.

"There's the girls." Reaper says with a smile looking to our left.

Turning in that direction, I see Britni not far behind them trying to keep up but the crowd is so thick she seems to be losing sight of Jade and Fire.

I see her mouth move as if to call to the girls but they don't seem to hear her over all the music and the rest of the crowd.

Britni's eyes get a wild look about them as she scans the faces walking past her. Something about her fear clearly registering on her face has my feet moving in her direction before I even think about it.

I see her shoulders go stiff as she stares straight ahead of her but I can't see whatever it is she's looking at.

As I get closer, I call her name but she never looks in my direction, not even when I'm within feet of her so I grab her shoulder.

The scream she lets loose has the crowd stopping to look at us both. I spin her to face me and shake her a little.

"It's me! You're okay. It's just me." Her eyes clear as she looks into my face before wrapping her arms around me and burrowing her face into my chest.

"What was that about?" I ask, wondering what in the fuck just happened.

She raises her face to look back at me.

"I'm sorry. I just got scared when I couldn't find anyone I knew." She answers but I see her once again look back behind her.

I scan the faces but don't see anything out of the ordinary. Looking back into her beautiful face, I glide my index finger along her face from her ear to her chin, lifting it to my lips for a chaste kiss.

"You know I'd never let anything happen to you, right?"

She looks at me with her brows drawn as if she's trying to figure me out but doesn't say anything back.

"Come on. I'm sure the Prez and everyone else is waiting for us." I take her hand into my own as we turn back the way I came.

"Why would they wait?" She asks curiously.

"Because we're family and we like to eat together." I smile, turning to look at her, not admitting that the Prez has ordered that no one actually go off completely alone.

Before turning my head back to the front I once again notice the Demon Riders standing not far off. Both looking directly at the two of us and one in particular with a grin on his face.

Deciding to just turn away, we carry on back towards my family. I should probably tell Reaper about that little encounter even though it was only a look. Those assholes are up to something. Wherever there are Demon Riders, there's trouble soon to follow.

Britni

After eating with the rest of the men and women of the club, everyone came back to the campers and sat around a bonfire for a while just talking.

Grease and I finally head inside around midnight.

Climbing in the bed next to him, I lay my head on his chest just feeling the rise and fall as he breathes.

It seems to finally calm me after the scare earlier in the day.

I know they saw me and recognized me. I heard them call out my real name.

Having already been scared that I was lost in the crowd, seeing those two standing there with a grin, scared me even more.

If they had grabbed me, would anyone have done anything to stop them from taking me even if I was screaming?

No one made a move when I screamed after Grease grabbed my shoulder although I didn't know it was him until I turned around.

"Hey. You okay? You've been more quiet this evening than I've known you to be." Grease asks while rubbing my back lazily.

"Just tired." I yawn right at the same time giving the lie a small shred of truth. "Will we head back home tomorrow?" I ask, changing the subject.

"Yeah. There's one last huge party. More like a send off party before everyone leaves."

I sigh loudly. "Another party?"

He chuckles, "No worries. I don't want to go either so I thought we'd take my bike and go for a long ride. Meet everyone back here by the afternoon so we can all ride home together."

"You came in the truck though." I look up at him, confused.

"One of the prospects that was pulling a big enclosed trailer brought the bikes of the guys who drove in the cages on the way here."

"Cages?" I laugh. "That's what you call a vehicle?" I try to act dumb when it comes to these things not wanting him to know that I'm familiar with motorcycle clubs.

"You're a nurse. Does it not seem like a cage to you?"

Thinking on it for a minute, I do see his point. "Yeah, I guess it is."

"Exactly. Now, let's get some sleep, woman. I'll need to make sure this camper is all packed up and ready to pull out when we get back before we leave on our ride in the morning." He whispers back, sounding more sleepy than even I am.

Snuggling closer into the crook of his arm, his hand moves down cupping my ass.

"God, I love that ass." He whispers, giving it a few good squeezes.

Although I've been afraid all evening, here wrapped up in his arms, I relax until I fall asleep.

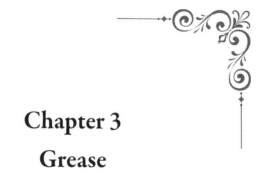

Chapter 3
Grease

"You sure you guys don't want to come to the party, man? It's always a fucking blast!" Aero chuckles at his own little joke.

"I'm sure besides some of the shit that goes on there just might scare Britni. I've done really well this past week in hiding most of the craziness." I say, remembering a few nights ago when I steered her in another direction just so she wouldn't see the two men with one woman pinned between them going at it like rabbits.

She'd have probably ran for the hills that very night and ignored me for the rest of her life.

A lot of the unattached and even some of the attached women that come to these things like to be shared with some of the other brothers.

Their old men are perfectly fine with all of it. Some join in and some just want to watch as another takes what's theirs.

I don't understand it either. There's no way in hell I could ever share my woman with another. I'm no Saint and yes I have shared other women. Women that were unattached and looking for something more than just missionary.

Although those wild and crazy days have been far behind me for a lot of years.

These days I prefer trying to take my time. Enjoy the moment. At least until the woman opens her mouth and starts talking. By then I'm ready to move on. Not with Britni though. I actually enjoy her company.

"I'm not sure this ride you are planning is a good idea without some of your brothers with you but I'm not going to use my position as your Prez to make you stay." Reaper comes from around the corner as I shut and lock the R.V. door.

"You worry too much, Prez." I grin at the young man I've watched become one of the best Presidents of our club.

"Just check-in alright? Otherwise be back here by three. That's when I plan to roll out."

"Will do!" I slap him on the shoulder and head off in search of Britni.

I've thought about it all morning and know exactly where I'd like to take her today. It's beautiful there and it'll give us some more time to talk. I still know so very little about her and I find myself wanting to know everything.

Britni

"Where are you two planning to ride to?" Jade asks as we take down the tables our crew put together for everyone to sit outside the campers.

"He didn't say anything specific." I shrug my shoulders.

"Well there's plenty of places to go around here that's beautiful."

"In the city?" I ask.

"Sure." She shrugs. "There's a few places along the coast not far from here that are amazing. Just make sure to enjoy yourself. I worry about you." She puts one of the folded tables into the truck and turns to look directly at me.

"Why would you worry about me?" I laugh, handing my table to one of the guys. I don't know what his name is as several of them all have Prospect on their cuts.

"You've just been, I don't know, off the last few days. I'm not sure what it is. Is it Grease? Is he being a dick?" She narrows her eyes.

"No." I laugh again. "Grease is...." I trail off, then turn to walk back to the last table waiting to be taken down.

"Oh no you don't. Finish that sentence." Jade runs after me.

"Well, he's pretty amazing actually." I sigh.

"And that's a problem?" Her brows pull together.

"Not really. It's just…"

"Stop doing that!" She demands, grabbing my arm to stop me where I am. "You always start to say what's on your mind then it's like pulling teeth to get you to finally say it. Just spit out exactly what you are feeling. Never hide it! Not from me and not from Grease." She looks hard into my eyes until I nod my head.

Turning to look at the last table, she looks back towards the truck and motions for one of the guys to come over.

"Finish that table up for us please." She tells him with a smile and I swear the boy falls over himself to do her bidding.

"You are so wrong for that." I chuckle.

"It comes with the territory of being the Big Boss Man's wife." She laughs. "Now, you were saying? What's the issue?"

"I keep wondering how long it can possibly last." I say in a rush.

"The relationship? Well no one can really answer that other than time."

"No. I mean him being so amazing. He's super nice. I'd almost call him a gentleman." I snort at the picture that puts in my mind. "A gentleman biker." I really start laughing once that is out of my mouth.

Jade can't hold it in either as she begins to snort right along with me. That's how Grease finds us. Both bent at the waist trying to hold the other up as we laugh, then snort, then laugh even more because we snorted.

"Sometimes women are so fucking weird." We hear Reaper even though we can't see out of our watery eyes.

"Weird? They look like they've lost their fucking minds." Grease murmurs sending us into another snorting fit.

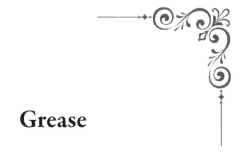

Grease

C oming to a stop, I kill the engine before helping her from the back of my bike. As soon as she's off she pulls her helmet off and sighs.

"This is beautiful!" She spins around looking in every direction.

Looking along the West End of Dauphin Island, the white sand glimmers in the sunlight. I've always loved this place. The entire Island is beautiful no matter what time of year you visit.

"So you've never been here?" I grin at her huge smile.

"No. I've heard of the island but didn't think something this beautiful could be so close to the United States without having to get on a plane or boat." She laughs.

"Well technically, you could come by boat. There's a ferry."

"Really? I bet that would be an amazing trip."

"It is but there's no time for it today. Come on, let's walk." I turn back towards my bike, opening the saddlebags before I reach for my zipper on my jeans.

"What are you doing?" She gasps.

"Taking my pants off."

"Why? This isn't a nude beach. Wait, is it a nude beach?" She asks, quickly looking at all the other people around.

I can't stop from laughing at her. "I'm not getting naked. I have shorts underneath."

Grabbing the middle of her chest with her right hand she sighs in relief. "Oh, thank God because if this was a nude beach you were totally going it alone!"

"Seriously? You'd let me flash all my wares to everyone around?"

"You're the one they'd be laughing at." She throws her hand over her mouth just as quickly as she says it and fear reaches her eyes.

Instead of the reaction I suspect she thought she'd get I let out a booming laugh that has others turning to look in our direction.

Taking my pants the rest of the way off, I fold them and lay them in my saddlebags before turning back to her.

Her eyes give her away. She's still afraid of what she said. I suspect from the things I've noticed this past week, someone has made her afraid of speaking her mind to the point she doesn't even like to joke.

Whoever the fucker is, he best hope I never get the chance to meet him.

"I brought us both some flip flops to wear." I pull them from my bag, handing her the smallest pair.

After we put them on and place our boots into the bags, I grab her hand and we start off towards the beach.

"I wish you wouldn't look at me like that." I say after several long minutes of silence between us.

"Like what?" She looks up at me.

"Like you're afraid of me. It doesn't matter what it is, you can always be who you are with me. If you feel like I need a good smack upside the head. Then do it. You never have to worry about me raising a hand to you. Not ever." I hold her eyes with mine hoping she can see how very sincere I am.

"I'll try to be better." She finally says.

"I don't want you to try to be better. I just want you to be who you are." I pull us both to a stop at the water's edge.

She stares back at me for several long moments and I just hold her eyes with my own.

"You really are kind of amazing, huh." She whispers, inching closer to me.

"Not really. I just don't think a woman should ever have to be scared of a man. At least not one she is in a relationship with." I grin.

"A relationship? We have a relationship?" She inches even closer until she's flush against me and my hands automatically go to her ass.

"Well, yeah. I love this ass." I give it a good squeeze. "It fits me perfectly."

She giggles just as I take her mouth with my own.

Britni

Today was a good day. I really enjoyed the time we spent walking along the beach shore, picking up shells and just talking about everything under the sun.

Sitting back, enjoying the ride as we head back to meet up with everyone else, I think back over our conversations.

He told me all kinds of silly stories about the men in his club. Some of which I find extremely hard to believe. That many big burly bikers all in one place, surely there's a few bad seeds in the lot.

I tried to answer his questions about my own life as best I could without giving away too much. I've found that sticking to the truth as closely as possible makes it a lot easier to keep everything straight.

Telling him about growing up in a group home was easier than I'd thought it would be. Most people who've ever heard that look at me with pity.

He, however, didn't do that. Instead he just asked me about what it was like, the things we did as kids, if the people were nice.

I know the stories of kids growing up in other places similar to the place I was in or even in foster care. There's news headlines almost daily about the shady practices behind the

41

scenes. However, where I grew up was almost magical and I hated to leave once I became of age.

Before this mess I found myself in, I stayed in touch with the headmistress there and I often wonder if she thinks of me, wondering why she's not heard from me in so long.

She caught me breaking into her office once when I was twelve, determined to find out who my real parents were. I remember sitting there in her office as she stared a hole at me until I finally told her why I was breaking in.

After explaining to me all the ways in why what I did was wrong, she sent me to my room where I was to stay for a week, having my supper by myself instead of with the other kids.

It wasn't until I was aging out that I found out a little more. There technically were no records for me as I was found by a good Samaritan in a trash can with my umbilical cord still attached and wet with blood.

There was an investigation back then of course but the cops never found out anything about where I came from.

One day I'd like to visit the town where I was found which is only a short drive outside of Bozeman Montana. While I have no illusions of finding out who my family is all these years later, I'd still like to see the place where my family is possibly from.

We're just coming up to a stop sign when I feel Grease's hand on my leg tighten differently. I'm turning my head to look in the direction that he's looking when I hear screeching tires. I never get a look at the vehicle as I feel myself flying through the air and within seconds the world goes dark.

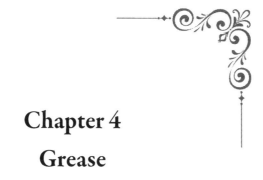

Chapter 4
Grease

The doctors and nurses had to threaten me to keep me in this bed as all I wanted to do was follow where they were taking Britni.

The truck that hit us, sent us both flying through the air in separate directions. I landed hard on my left side and heard when the bone in my arm broke.

Although in excruciating pain, I immediately rolled, jumping to my feet just in case the fuckers in the truck tried to run me completely over with the tires.

The truck screeched off just as I was getting up but I couldn't see a license plate. There was no doubt in my mind this was a planned hit but to what purpose I just don't know yet.

I scanned the area trying to find Britni and finally spotted her in some tall weeds about twenty yards away from.

Rushing to her side, I could see her helmet had cracked and there was blood oozing from a gash on her forehead.

As I tried to revive her, I called for an ambulance. Her breathing was erratic but at least she was breathing.

The nurse is just finishing up on my cast when my Prez walks into the room with a pissed off look that has several people moving out of his way.

"Thank fuck you are alright!" He booms out just as Jade rushes in behind him.

"Jesus, you scared us, Grease!" She places her hand over her chest, breathing hard.

"I told you when I called that I was fine." I raise my brows.

"You don't look fine to me! You look like a beat up old man." Loki says lazily from the door.

"Your family I presume?" The nurse asks with a small grin.

"Yeah. Can always count on that one there to be an asshole in any situation." I nod towards Loki.

"Well we are almost finished here and then you can go visit your wife." She says softly from next to me.

I see my Prez raise his brows slightly at the wife bit but no one corrects the woman about who Britni is to me.

"Can you tell me if she's woken up yet?" I ask.

"I honestly don't know. They have her on the upper floor. In room three twelve." She finishes up, collecting her things.

"Thanks." I say as she wades through my brothers, heading for the door.

"Wife?" Prez asks as soon as she's gone.

"They assumed and I didn't correct them. Britni told me she doesn't have any family and I figured if they thought I was her husband I could ask all the damn questions I wanted without getting put off."

Prez shakes his head in understanding as we all head towards the door although I walk a bit more stiffly. As I walk out the nurse is back with a fucking wheelchair.

"Sorry Mr. Gaige but it's hospital policy."

"If you insist on calling me something, then call me Ja'sin." I roll my eyes as I plop down into the chair.

Prez just shakes his head while Loki outright laughs at me having to sit in a chair that is pushed by someone else.

"I'll take him unless there's some rule that you have to do it?" Jade asks the nurse sweetly, taking over the chair.

"Elevators are just down the hall. I hope your wife is okay Mr. Ja'sin." The nurse says, walking away.

"Can't believe you didn't invite us to the wedding." Loki grins as we step into the elevator.

"If you don't shut the fuck up, you won't make it to tomorrow." I growl.

"Loki, there's no time for your games. We need to see how Britni is doing then figure out if this was a hit and run or something more." Prez quietly says with authority.

"Yeah, that's what scares me." Jade quietly says.

"Don't worry baby. Everything will be fine." He pulls her closer, kissing her on the head.

Coming out of the elevator we make our way to the nurse's desk to check in.

"You can go on down to her room. I'll send the doctor down there to talk to you." The nurse says kindly, pointing down the hall.

Getting to the door, I make Jade stop the chair so I can get out. I can walk into that room by myself for fucks sake. I may be stiff and sore from the wreck but I ain't fucking dead yet.

Opening the door, the first thing I notice is that she looks like she's sleeping. There's multiple wires going from her to all kinds of machines that are beeping but she's definitely still breathing on her own.

Her face is all bruised and battered with small cuts. The gash she had on her forehead is sewn together with stitches.

It's fairly straight and should heal without too much of a scar left that'll fade even more with time.

Grabbing her hand in mine, I expect her to wake up immediately but she doesn't. Even her heart monitor continues its steady beat.

"Mr. Gaige?" A voice from the door has me turning to find the doctor walking into the room.

"Yes?" I answer, waiting.

"Your wife had a significant hit to the head although there's been no swelling of her brain which we are still monitoring. She didn't appear to have any broken bones either or internal injuries." He says looking at me,

"Then why isn't she awake?" I ask, confused.

"The brain is a complex thing that we still don't know everything about even in this day and age. I'd say she'll wake up on her own eventually as to when that'll be I can't really say. Currently it's a waiting game."

"So she's fine other than she's just not waking up? Does that mean she's in a coma?" Jade asks.

"In a way. Yes. She may wake up tomorrow or it could be weeks from now. We just don't know. I'm sorry."

My heart beats fast at the realization that this beautiful woman may be like this for a long time.

The one woman I've found that I truly enjoy being with. The one woman that I could see myself living forever with.

"Fucking life is a fickle bitch." I whisper as the doctor leaves.

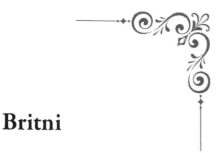

Britni

Opening my eyes, I don't understand where I'm at. A beeping sound from next to me draws my eyes and I look over to find a machine with wires that I'm hooked up to.

I'm in a hospital, I realize but can't remember how I got here. I'm in the middle of trying to remember what happened when the door swings open and a nurse walks in. She's next to the bed before she looks at me.

"Oh, sweet girl. You're awake! Your husband will be so glad to know it!" She hurriedly checks my vitals.

"My husband?" I croak through my dry lips.

"You're probably so thirsty. Hang on, I'll get you a little water." She grabs a cup with a straw, holding it to my mouth.

The water isn't very cold but it's wet and feels wonderful as it makes its way down my throat.

"Why am I here?" I ask, letting go of the straw.

"You and your husband had an accident on that motorcycle of his. Those things are dangerous, you know." She says quickly but my mind once again grabs on to the husband bit.

"I've never ridden a motorcycle before and I certainly don't have a husband." I look at her with confusion.

"What's the last thing you remember honey?" She asks gently.

I open my mouth to respond but nothing comes out. Nothing comes to mind about anything. Oh my god, I can't even remember my name. I have a name. Don't I? Of course I do!

Holy shit. My breathing comes faster in my chest as it tightens on the air I'm taking in. My eyes begin to water and I know the nurse is talking fast to me but I don't hear a single thing for several long moments.

"Breathe slowly! That's it. In and out. You just had a little panic attack is all." She talks calmly to me.

The door to my room opens quickly once again and a doctor walks in.

"Our patient is finally awake I see." He smiles but the nurse hurries over to him whispering quickly. "I see." His eyes draw together before he turns back to me.

"I understand you're having a little trouble remembering but that is okay. You were bumped on the head pretty badly so temporary memory loss isn't completely unexpected." He explains, walking over to my bedside. "Nurse, go out to the nurses desk and call her husband. Maybe that will make you feel a little better. Hm?"

Make me feel better? A man that is supposedly my fucking husband but I can't even remember him? I can't even remember what the hell my own name is, much less a husband!

"My name. What's my name?" I ask quickly, my heart still racing uncontrollably.

"Britni Gaige, dear. Trust me and don't panic, alright?" He smiles gently.

Less than five minutes later, my door opens once again to reveal an older man that is probably the sexiest man alive although I really wouldn't know at this point considering I don't remember a fucking thing.

"I'm glad you still think so, beautiful." He grins and I realize I said that out loud.

He walks straight up to my bed without stopping to acknowledge the doctor or nurse.

"I'm so fucking glad to see those eyes of yours. You had me scared." He whispers, leaning down to kiss my still dry lips gently.

I don't move from the kiss and something about it seems right even though I don't remember him.

"Mr. Gaige, your wife is having some memory loss. I'm pretty confident that it's temporary so I don't want either of you to worry too much about it. I'm not saying it won't make things a little hard on you but I have every reason to believe that she will regain those memories."

Mr. Gaige, since that's the only name I know him as so far, looks back at me with concern on his face.

"You don't remember the accident sweetheart?" He asks gently, skimming his finger along my jaw line.

"I don't remember anything." I whisper, my heart rate accelerating once again.

"Anything? As in the accident or..." He asks.

"Or. Definitely or." I swallow hard.

"Oh fuck." He straightens up quickly. "How long will this last?" He asks the doctor, moving slightly away from me but grabbing my hand.

I'm thankful for that small little link between us. I drown out the conversation going on around me as I concentrate on his hand being in mine. It feels right as if it's something we've done millions of times. Maybe this one thing is all I can remember but at least it's something.

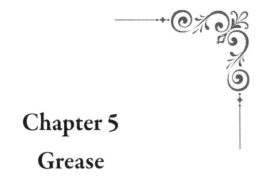

Chapter 5
Grease

For the past four days I've stayed close to Britni in the hospital. My Prez and other brothers have stayed in the area as well.

Each of them takes turns to be here at the hospital to keep an eye out as well as to make sure I eat.

That last bit is probably more Jade's doing. She's always been the little mother-hen when it comes to us men in the club even though a lot of us are older than she is.

Especially me. Hell, It wouldn't be too much of a stretch to say I'm old enough to be her father.

Britni has asked quite a lot of questions in the past few days.

Some of which I've been unable to answer for her.

I'm pretty sure she's beginning to wonder how the hell her so-called husband doesn't know that much about her but I've been able to put her off by being truthful.

She grew up in a children's home and has no family beyond me and the club.

Yeah, I'm probably a dick for not telling her the truth about us not being married but even Jade thought it might be too much for Britni to process just yet.

"Has the doctor been around yet today?" The Prez asks as I take a seat next to him on a bench outside the hospital.

The nurses were taking Britni for a few new scans and I didn't see any point sitting in her room by myself, twiddling my damn thumbs.

"Not yet. He's supposed to be around later after these new scans. Nurse seems to think he'll be releasing her to go home." I grumble.

"Well, that's a good thing. We need to get back to our home turf and figure this shit out. I want to know who the fuck ran you two down and why." Prez growls.

"I've been thinking about that. I don't think this is actually a hit at the club but a hit at her." I nod towards the hospital.

"You telling me you think that sweet little woman has someone out for her?" He looks at me with raised brows.

"I know how it sounds with knowing what little we do know of her but that is part of it too. We know very little about her. Even though I know very little. She never told much and I honestly think what she did tell me was truthful. You know I can see through any bullshit."

"That's true. So what do we know?" He asks.

"She was raised in a children's group home." I say, ticking off one finger.

"Where's the group home?" He asks.

"No fucking clue. There's also the way she was at the rally. She saw something or someone that scared her and I've also noticed that when I would call her name sometimes in the crowds, she didn't seem to recognize her own name."

"Maybe she changed her name." He states and I shake my head.

"Question would be why? Why would she need to change her name? And change the way she looks." His eyes widen.

"Change her looks, how?" He asks.

"You've not been up to see her since that first day but her hair has grown out some showing roots that are clearly not as red as the rest of it. It's more of a brown color." I say, staring up at the hospital windows, wondering if they are done with their tests yet.

"Anything new as far as her getting her memories back?" He asks.

"Nothing yet. I'm hoping when we get her back home to North Mississippi, something will just click for her."

"It could make shit a hell of a lot easier, that's for fucking sure."

"Yeah. Where's Jade?" I ask, changing the subject.

"Her and the other girls wanted a day at the beach."

"You didn't want to go?" I ask with a grin.

"And get fucking sand in my boots like last year and get my feet all fucked up with blisters on the way home? Hell no!"

"That's why you wear flip flops. You looked fucking ridiculous with boots on the beach in a pair of shorts last year."

"At least my feet weren't burnt to a crisp for a week after like the rest of you stupid fuckers."

I laugh at the memory of that. The rest of us all complained after getting back home.

We couldn't even wear our boots at work as they rubbed the sunburned skin too badly and when you work in a garage, anything other than boots is not worth the risk.

"I better head back up. See if we know when we can leave or not." I stand up from the bench.

"Let me know. We're ready just as soon as you are." Prez says as I walk back to the hospital.

I wasn't lying to the Prez about thinking hard over everything. Even at the rally something kept niggling at the back of my brain that something was off with Britni.

While I don't think she's been completely up front with me, I also don't think she's out right lied either.

She doesn't seem like the type to be that devious. I know what devious looks like when I see it. I didn't get to be VP of this club for nothing.

Britni

J a'sin came back to my room just a few minutes after the nurses brought me back from all the tests they wanted to run. I've noticed he stays on his phone a lot, sending text messages.

He doesn't tell me who he's talking to and I don't ask. There seems to be a lot of secrets between my husband and I.

I still can't get over the fact that I have a husband or that there's some things that I do remember like the scar on the inside of my thigh I got from falling off my bike as a kid.

Ja'sin has explained to me that he's part of a motorcycle club and that we live in North Mississippi.

We were apparently down here for some kind of rally. We were coming back from the beach when we were hit by another vehicle.

I know that it's got to be frustrating to have a wife that doesn't even remember you just as it's frustrating for me to not remember him.

He seems like a really good guy though. What little we've been able to talk here in the hospital. I just wish I could remember our life from before.

"Are you ready to go home my dear?" The doctor asks with a smile as he comes into the room.

"I can go home?" I smile, looking over at Ja'sin.

"Yes, you can but I expect you to go see your regular doctor by next week so they can continue your care from here. You need to be monitored even after you regain your memories."

"You sure she's up for this? That she can travel?" Ja'sin asks.

"Absolutely. All her scans came back as normal. She has no bleeds, no swelling, she's completely healthy minus the bruises she still has."

"How soon will you be releasing her?"

"The nurses should be in here within the next hour for you to sign all your paperwork." The Doctor answers before turning back to me. "I want to wish you luck Mrs. Gaige. You are truly a miracle."

"A miracle without memories." I grumble.

"I have complete faith you will get those back and if you don't? Just make some new ones. The point is to enjoy life as fully as possible."

After the doctor leaves, Ja'sin steps out to make a few calls while I get dressed to leave. While we may be married, it still feels too weird for me to be naked around him.

"Knock, knock!"

I spin around to the door to see the woman that was here with Ja'sin the day I opened my eyes. She was with a man that was wearing the same type of leather vest that Ja'sin never seems to take off.

"Hello." I smile slightly at her.

"It's really good to see you up and around. Reaper and Grease refused to allow me back up here once they knew you couldn't remember much." She says in a rush as she comes further into the room.

"Reaper and Grease?" I lift my brows having no idea who she means.

"Oh, guess you aren't familiar with the names. Reaper is the President of the club. Grease is what we call Ja'sin."

"Why would you call him that? Is that his nickname? And what kind of name is Reaper?" I'm getting more confused by the second.

The woman laughs then sticks her hand out. "Let's start over. I'm Jade and I'm a friend of yours. We've not known each other too long but long enough to know we are definitely friends. Reaper is my husband and the names of the guys are what's called road names."

Taking her hand, I shake it with a smile.

"Guess I have a lot of catching up to do." I shrug.

"It's okay. Just take your time. There's no reason to rush. So I hear you get to go home today which is good, I'm ready to get home myself."

"Ja'sin mentioned that you all stayed. Why didn't you all go on home instead of staying down here?"

"Because of the number one rule of the club. Club family means everything and you are part of the club family."

Her use of the word family makes my heart jump a little in my chest and I wonder if it's because of Ja'sin explaining to me that I grew up in a group home.

Not having any family as a child, I guess I grew up and found one. The thought makes me smile.

"There's that smile. Now, I brought you some clothes so you wouldn't have to wear whatever the hospital has found for you to wear." She hands me a bag and I peep inside.

"This is perfect! Thank you, Jade." I pull her in for a hug and she automatically hugs me back.

I can't stop the tears that begin rolling down my cheeks and she holds me a little tighter.

"You're going to be okay. We are all here for you." She whispers.

Grease

"You take her home with you, Duh." Loki rolls his eyes.

"We aren't actually married though!" I protest, looking over at my Prez hoping he'll give me some insight into what I should do here.

We all have basically lied for over a week now that she is my wife. She's even listed as such at the hospital she's been staying at.

Although, we've not had to claim anything with an insurance company because I paid straight cash for every bit of her medical bills, I'm sure there's some law we've broken by doing so.

"Look." Prez sighs. "She still doesn't remember anything. I've talked to Dr. Ortez. You remember him right?"

"Yeah. He's with the Wolfsbane club out in Montana."

"He believes that it wouldn't do her any favors to tell her the truth right now. Says it could hinder her healing process. She's used to you being there at this point so what's done is done. She'll go home with you."

"What about the rest of the club? They'll need to know what's going on."

"Loki and I will take care of that. You just go get your girl ready to go. I'll have Bones bring over a cage for the two of you to ride back in."

As I head back to her room, I meet Jade in the hallway.

"She doing alright?" I ask.

"Seems fine other than the memory bit. I can still see her in there. The woman she was before all this. If you know what I mean." She says, looking back towards Britni's door.

"I know exactly what you mean." I answer, remembering the first night I actually took my shirt off before laying on the extra bed the hospital brought in for me.

The look in her eyes when she looked at me had my cock wanting to snap to attention. Took me far longer than it should have to fall asleep that night, sleeping on my side so she wouldn't see the tent I was pitching in the bed.

"The nurse just finished getting her to sign all the discharge papers so I guess I'll see you guys out front soon." I nod my head at her as she walks away and I turn to Britni's door.

Continuing this charade of me being her husband feels so wrong to me. I hate lying and being forced to do so is fucking killing me.

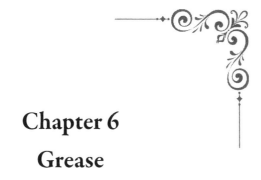

Chapter 6
Grease

We've been home for several days now and it still feels so weird coming home to a woman in my house. Although I do have to admit that it's been really nice.

Other than asking why we didn't have any pictures on the walls, she's not asked too many questions about our lives together.

Jade made sure to call ahead before we all got back home to get Joanna, Bone's wife, to bring some clothes over here and put them in the closet, as well as some girly shit in the bathroom.

I'm thankful she thought of it, otherwise there's no way I could have explained how my so-called wife lives here but doesn't have a stitch of clothing in the entire damn house.

Britni's stayed in the house since we got here other than the day she had an appointment with the local doctor that she was referred to.

On the second day, she realized that she knew how to cook and something is always waiting for me now when I come in from work.

I tried to tell her that I didn't expect her to cook for me but she wouldn't hear of it, claiming it's the one thing she seems to have some memory of even though it wasn't in our kitchen.

One of these days I'm likely to come in and have whatever magnificent dinner she's made that day thrown at my head because she's regained her memories. There's no way for her to not be completely pissed off at me for lying about that and that is what scares me.

I've come to realize in the last couple of days that she means more to me than I've let my brothers even know.

Even when she finally remembers everything, she can be pissed at me but I will be damned if I let her run for me.

We need to see where our relationship can go. I'm not getting any younger and I refuse to live the rest of my life with regrets like letting her leave me before we really even get a good start.

This whole accident thing is just a bump in the road. While it sucks big fucking cocks, it's better that it's happened now instead of years from now.

What if we had been married when she lost her memory?

What if we had children together that she couldn't even remember giving birth to?

I couldn't imagine trying to explain such a thing to a child. It would be devastating for everyone, especially the child.

There's been a lot of meetings with all the guys of the club as we try to figure out if it really was a regular hit and run or something more sinister. If someone's coming after the club, we need to know about it.

Walking into the house, the smell of a roast hits my senses making my mouth water and my stomach growl loudly.

"I guess you're hungry. I could hear that from here." Britni giggles from the door leading into the kitchen.

Looking at her, I'm once again hit with how beautiful she is. Standing there at that moment in a tank top with a pair of super short shorts that I don't remember her having.

"Where'd you get the shorts?" I ask, my eyes still glued to the smooth skin of her thighs.

"Jade stopped by earlier. Said she was throwing me a welcome home party this weekend and brought me some clothes she said she was just going to throw out." She answers with a shrug, turning back into the kitchen taking the wonderful view of those thighs away.

Throwing all my shit down by the front door, I follow her into the kitchen. I wonder if she'd let me close enough to run the tips of my fingers on that silky smooth skin?

"Why are you staring?" Her question snaps me out of my daze and I look up into her eyes.

The grin on her face tells me she knows exactly what I was staring at. Possibly even knows what I was thinking. Not wanting to scare her though, I've kept my distance even though it's been hard as fuck to sleep in my room while she's just across the hall.

"Dinner ready?" I ask after clearing my throat. Hopefully I can sit across from her and eat without staring a hole through her tank top, imagining her tits in my mouth.

Britni

I've been tossing and turning for an hour now. Last night I woke up from a dream that felt more like a memory.

I was in the shower and he came in completely naked, pressing himself into me from behind.

Thinking about it now, my body feels hot all over and I'm getting slick between my legs.

Unable to help myself, I run my fingers over my own nipples, giving them a pinch that sends electricity to my throbbing clit.

Closing my eyes I can imagine my hands as those of Ja'sin sliding down my stomach straight to the one place I need the most attention.

As my hand glides over my clit, my ass lifts from the bed pushing my center more firmly into my hand.

Slicking my fingers with my own wetness, I rub small steady circles over my clit, working up to a faster speed.

I can feel myself climbing higher but just unable to reach the precipice that will send me over the edge.

Working my hand faster, increasing my pace and even pinching my nipple hard with the other hand only heightens the thrumming in my body instead of relieving it.

Frustrated beyond belief, I lay there panting, balling the sheet into my hand and wonder if it's seriously possible for a woman to get the equivalent of blue balls.

I think very seriously of walking across the hall and crawling into bed with my husband.

Would he willingly give me what I want? I was honestly surprised he suggested I sleep across the hall instead of in our marital bed.

I know that we are essentially starting over but does he not want me that way any more? Maybe we didn't have a very good sex life before?

That can't be it though. Not with the dreams I've been having of us together. They feel too real to not be memories.

He's been very sweet to me and seems to go out of his way just for me. I've had a feeling that coming home after work every single day isn't something he's used to doing. That's why I asked Jade about it today.

She said that we usually ate with the rest of the club at the clubhouse. All the women would get together there to cook everything and everyone would sit down to eat together. Like a family is supposed to.

It's a tradition they all started as soon as Reaper took over the club. He wanted all the members and their kids to know that family was the most important thing in the world.

That's one of the reasons I'm looking forward to the welcome home party she's throwing for me this weekend.

Maybe Ja'sin and I can get back into our regular routine of family dinners. Besides, it would be nice to have more people to talk to.

I've been considering asking my husband if I could possibly get a dog. I found several ads for puppies in the paper that came in the mail today.

I could go ask him now since I know he'll be gone before I get up in the morning.

My body once again starts to hum at the thought of seeing him laying in bed. I wonder if he sleeps naked? My clit throbs at the thought.

Yes. I'll go ask him now. About the puppy that is. And if he's naked, even better.

I jump up out of bed, pulling my shirt back down as I head for the door.

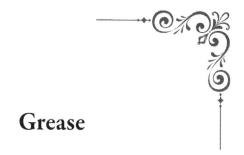

Grease

I've not been sleeping very well the past week. It's as if my entire body knows that she is directly across the hall from me and I usually don't fall asleep until after midnight.

The shit is taking a toll on me as I snapped at one of the Walker boys at the shop today over something as trivial as not getting me the tires I needed for the bike I was working on fast enough.

Even the Prez has looked at me like I've lost my fucking mind but he's not said anything to me about my behavior yet.

He knows me well enough to know that I'm probably beating myself up over it enough and he doesn't need to say anything at all.

Tossing myself over onto my back, I sigh into the darkness just as I hear the small sound of my door knob turning.

Looking towards the door, Britni's face appears in the moonlight shining through the open window and I raise up on the bed.

"Britni? Everything okay?" I ask worriedly.

"Um...Yes. I just wanted to ask you something." She whispers back even though we are the only two here.

"Okay." I sit up even straighter, keeping the covers over my waist.

She comes further into the room until she's an arms length away, right next to the bed. She stares hard at me through the darkness and I wonder briefly what she's looking for as her eyes seem to scan me from my head to my waist.

"You want to sit down?" I ask, scooting over to make room for her on the bed, thinking she'll sit just on the edge.

Instead, she sits but turns, laying back against the headboard with her feet up on the bed and I swear I've never seen anything more beautiful in my life. I sit back too but try to keep the blanket bunched up over my now rock hard cock.

Turning my head in her direction, I once again see that she's staring right at me. Has she remembered something?

Just as I'm about to ask her, she leans over quickly pressing her lips to mine in a chaste kiss that still has the ability to set this room into a blaze.

She breaks the kiss first and I try not to move, afraid of scaring her so badly she runs screaming from the room.

"What was that for?" I finally ask, breaking the silence between us.

"I don't know." She shrugs, looking away. "I just felt like it."

Reaching up to her face slowly, I take her chin into my palm, turning her to look back at me.

"In that case then..." I whisper, leaning over and taking her mouth again with my own but this time, I run my tongue along her bottom lip until she gasps.

Running my tongue along hers, I take her mouth in the way I've been wanting to do since she first opened her eyes at the hospital. I continue my assault until she's moaning and her hands grab hold on my head, pulling me even closer.

Breaking off the kiss, the only sounds in the room are us both breathing heavily. My own body is screaming to pull her under me and show her how I feel about her in the most intimate way possible.

"Wow…" She finally whispers, her fingertips feeling her own lips.

Fuck yeah, wow. She's wowed me since the very first night we met. Having her with me now, every single day, I can no longer see me in this house without her.

"You wanted to ask me something?" I finally ask when my own breathing settles.

"Can I have a puppy?" Her question startles me as it was not the question that I expected.

"A puppy?"

"Yeah. I found some in the paper and I was wondering if I might have one. I've always wanted a puppy." Her last sentence seems to startle us both.

"Is that a memory?" I ask gently with a grin.

She looks contemplative for several long minutes until I think she's not going to answer.

"I think it is." She says quietly before a huge smile takes over her entire face.

There's no way in hell I can tell her no to getting a puppy when that is the very first thing she's been able to remember.

Not that I would tell her no anyway. It's not like she's asked for anything. Not even since we came home.

"A puppy would be great." I smile as her eyes get even bigger with excitement.

"Really?" She bounces on the bed.

"Really." I laugh at the girlishness she is exhibiting until she launches herself into my lap.

Now I can no longer laugh. All I can do is feel. Her entire body against my own. Something that I had no idea just how much I missed until this very moment. Apparently my cock didn't forget though.

We stay just like that in my bed, talking for at least another hour about the puppy she's going to get until she falls asleep in my arms.

Not wanting to pass up an opportunity to hold her in my arms, I lay her down on the bed next to me, pulling her close to my side.

I'm asleep not long after and actually wake up for work in a much better mood than I've been lately. Before I head out, I watch her sleeping on my pillow for several minutes before kissing her on top of her head.

Today is going to be an amazing fucking day. She's starting to remember something, albeit small, she slept in my bed last night and we're getting a puppy. Nothing can take this feeling away from me.

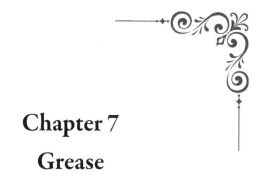

Chapter 7
Grease

Scanning the faces around me, I can't keep the smile from my face as I watch my entire club family enjoying the afternoon sun.

Kids are running around everywhere with water guns far enough away from the adults to stay out of trouble having already had a run in with the Prez himself.

The Prez called a huge meeting with the entire club a few days after we came back from down South, warning them all about Britni's memory loss and that she currently thinks we are married.

While they guys have given me shit about it, all in good fun, they've made sure to keep the secret under wraps.

Jade and her sister took care of the women knowing who all have taken right to Britni, pulling her into the family without any issues at all.

If I ever in my life had any doubts about the decisions I've made, today shows me that picking these people as my family was the best thing I've ever done.

Glancing over at the women where Britni is sitting with her new puppy, her eyes glance up to mine, smiling brightly.

Grinning back at her, I send her a wink before turning back towards the grill to flip the burgers.

"You look happy." Bones grunts causing me to jump as I hadn't realized he was there.

"You're gonna give me a damn heart attack sneaking up on me like that one of these days." I growl.

"Nah. You're still a young buck. That old ticker of yours will have you outliving us all." He chuckles. "Back to what I was saying, you look happy for once."

"What are you going on about? I'm always happy." I shake my head.

"Nope. You've been content but not happy. I've not seen you happy in a long ass time. That girl right there is the reason." He nods towards Britni and I look in her direction yet again. "Yep. I know that look."

"What look?" I look back at him wondering if he's going to get to the fucking point.

Bones has always been the serious one as well as his wife. If a couple was ever made for each other, it was those two.

"The same look I still give my sweet Joanna. Like you are amazed as hell and scared to hell all in one." He laughs, walking off again.

"Bones imparting words of wisdom?" Aero asks, watching Bones walk away.

"He was doing something, as for it being wisdom, who the hell knows."

A few minutes later the Prez joins us by the grill, handing both of us a new cold beer.

"Thought you could use this since you've not left the grill in a while."

"Thanks, Prez." I take it gratefully.

"I wanted to let you know that I called in some favors with Skeeter down in New Orleans. He's going to get Buzz to see what he can find out. Maybe there's some video footage out there of the accident somewhere. We need to know what exactly happened."

"I agree. Something about it all just doesn't sit right with me and I have this odd feeling that she is the key. I'm just not sure what the lock is yet." I nod in Britni's direction.

"Has she remembered anything yet?"

"Not really. Mostly small things like her always wanting a dog, and I think deep down somehow she remembers being with me from before." My brows draw together. "Then again that could just be wishful thinking."

"You wanting her to at least remember you in some small way shouldn't be discounted, Grease." Aero speaks up, surprising me and I look over at him but he just shrugs.

"He's right, you know. We all watched how you were with her at the rally. You were different, in a good way and I think this accident kinda put the breaks on something good for you. Just remember that we are all here for you. For you both." Prez says, drinking his beer.

"Well fuck. How the hell did everything get so fucking deep? I thought only women talked about feelings." Bud says from behind us all.

"When you get a woman in your life, you'll figure out real fast how to talk about your feelings." Prez says.

"Fuck that! I don't want no woman around all the time." He curls his nose up. "What about you, Hammer?" He looks over to one of the other guys in the club.

Hammer and I have never been exactly close but he's definitely someone I'd want on my side in a life or death situation.

"Not me." He shakes his head. "We'll leave that to all those stupid fucks standing over there." He nods towards all the other brothers who are currently running around with water guns of their own playing with the kids.

"Shit. Them mother fuckers would have to grow up first." Aero murmurs as we watch Loki jump out from behind a tree, screaming like a banshee as he super soaks the kids who are trying to sneak up on Chains who hadn't realized they were so close to his hiding spot.

At the exact moment the kids start screaming, Chains also jumps up screaming and slapping at his clothes.

It takes us several moments to realize his dumb ass has stirred up a yellow jacket nest and they are attacking him.

The kids watch the scene for only a moment before they take off in the opposite direction having learned their lesson already about the tiny jackass bugs that sting.

Loki, deciding that he should maybe help a brother out, turns his huge water gun on Chains who is now yelling for a totally different reason.

The yellow jackets must give up their own assault but Loki doesn't stop the spray of water he's aiming directly at Chains' face.

The water eventually runs out and Chains turns his eyes to our prankster of a brother.

Knowing what is coming for his ass now, Loki throws the gun in one direction as he runs in the other.

None of us can stop laughing long enough to even draw a breath as Chains takes off after him swearing vengeance the entire way.

"Fuck, I love this life!" I declare, wiping the tears from my own eyes.

A round of "Hear, Hear" is heard from everyone.

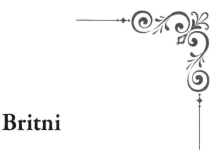

Britni

When we got to the clubhouse this afternoon for my welcome home party, I had a flash in my head of a scene almost similar but none of the faces in my head matched any of the people here. The clubhouse itself is different as well.

Maybe it's another place we've visited before for some reason? I've not mentioned it to Ja'sin yet as I don't want to spoil the party.

Everyone is having such a good time and I've enjoyed being around more women that I can talk to.

Not that I have much to say, preferring instead to listen to their conversations about the antics the kids have been getting up to.

I've had other memories the last few days as well that I've kept to myself. Mostly small pieces of time that I've had with Ja'sin.

In one memory, I called him Grease and have wondered if that is the name I always used instead of his given name.

He doesn't act like it bothers him that I call him Ja'sin but maybe I should ask him as I've noticed that Jade calls her husband Reaper. At least when everyone is around.

Is that a rule of the club that I should also be following?

My eyes glance over at him laughing with the other guys sitting at a table under a shade tree.

He's so damn handsome and I once again wonder how I got so lucky to have a husband like him.

He's been so patient with me about everything. Some things though he's been too patient.

I thought that once I got in his bed, he'd take the hint that I want a little more from him. Especially after he kissed me the way he did that first night I went into his room.

But every single night all he does is pull me close and I'm left to listen to his breathing slow until he's asleep. The entire time I feel like my body is on fire with wanting him.

I've decided that tonight is going to be the night I feel everything the way I felt in the dreams I've been having.

Dreams that I believe are memories, I just need to experience it though to make sure that is what they are, At least that is what I am telling myself.

Maybe I should just tell him flat out I want him to make love to me? I wonder what he'd do with that? I giggle out loud unwillingly.

"What are you over here giggling to yourself about?" Fire, Jade's sister asks from beside me.

"What my husband would do if I asked him for something?" I feel my face flame up.

"Something, huh?" She giggles too, knowingly. "He'd most likely jump your bones like a man starving to death."

"You think so?" I raise my brows.

"From the looks I've seen him shooting your way all afternoon, I'd say I know so."

I look back at Ja'sin, finding his eyes once again on me. I hadn't realized he's been looking at me in any particular way than normal.

"I don't know." I laugh, looking down at Lolly, my new puppy.

"Trust me on this. I know what I see and I see a man desperate to touch a toy that has been denied him lately. Give the man his toy back." She laughs.

Thinking over her words, I laugh too but think she may be right. I'll go after what I want. Besides, he does seem to like kissing me. Hopefully he likes and wants to do more.

My body shivers, more than ready for a release that it's craved for a week now.

Two hours later, after helping the girls clean up from our cookout, Ja'sin and I head back home.

I have butterflies in my stomach from thinking about him possibly turning me down tonight when we go to bed.

"You okay? You've been quiet since we left the clubhouse." Ja'sin asks, putting the truck in park.

Looking around I realize that we're in our driveway and I must have zoned out the entire way here.

"I'm okay." I finally answer, grabbing the door handle to get out.

Once we're inside, I'm even more jittery, unable to think of what I should do next.

I must stand in one spot for too long as Ja'sin grabs me by the shoulders, looking straight into my eyes.

"You're shaking like a leaf." He murmurs with concern.

"I'm just tired." I smile at him.

"Being gone for so long today probably wore you completely out. You can get a shower first and I'll get in after you then we both can go to bed."

"Alright." I smile even wider thinking that I can just walk into the bedroom completely naked. Surely he can't confuse what I want when I'm on full display for him.

"Go ahead. I'll lock up." He grins, kissing my lips quickly as he turns me towards the hall.

I hurry to the bathroom, turning the water on and stripping as fast as I can. The hot water spraying down on my head feels amazing but I try not to waste time. I rush through washing my body and a fast shave of my legs.

Although I rushed, I know at least twenty minutes have passed. I start to walk out with just the towel wrapped around me but remember that I need to brush my teeth so I turn back to the sink.

As soon as I'm finished, I dry my mouth and open the door, stepping directly into the bedroom with as big of a smile as I can muster.

Instead of being greeted by a surprised Ja'sin, I'm instead looking at a beautiful man sleeping soundly on the bed.

Deciding that tonight just isn't going to be the night, I find a shirt and slip it on as well as a fresh pair of panties.

Turning all the lights off, I crawl into the bed and curl up against him. It doesn't take long for sleep to find me as well.

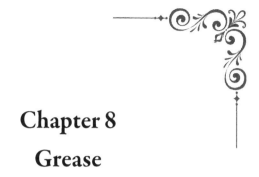

Chapter 8
Grease

I'm just walking out of the parts store when I hear my name being called.

Looking down the sidewalk I see a tiny little woman walking with a cane heading in my direction. With a grin, I wait for her close to the door.

"Afternoon, Mrs. Gibson." I greet her.

"Ja'sin Gaige, you get more handsome every time I see you. Just like your daddy."

My body stiffens at the mention of the man who was only good for one thing. Speeding his sperm all of the fucking country and disappearing into thin air.

"You need me to get the door for you?" I ask, trying to be polite.

"Don't dismiss me just yet, young man. I see the look on your face. Your daddy may have been rotten to the core but at least you got his looks. If I were just a tad younger, I'd jump your bones right here in the street! Yes sir!"

Shaking my head, I laugh at her antics. There's just no way to stay offended by a single thing she says because she will always make you laugh.

I also suspect she's being completely honest in everything she says. Even the bit about jumping my bones here in the street.

"If I was a tad bit older, I'd probably let you." I grin.

"Hot damn, I've still got it!" She pumps her arm and I laugh out loud.

Opening the door to the parts store, she moves towards the door.

"Oh. Tell those boys of yours to watch what they're doing. Almost ran me over."

"Wait." I stop her. "Where was this at?"

"Coming down past that old factory outside of town."

"Did you recognize who it was?" I ask, already planning the hard labor I'll dish out to any of the brothers caught not being careful where the locals are concerned.

"You know, these old eyes aren't what they once were, but I didn't recognize any of the faces. I figured you might have added some new boys to the group. Have a good day and come see me sometime." She reaches up, cupping my cheek.

"Hmmm." She shivers dramatically, turning and walking through the door as I'm left standing there laughing at her.

That woman was most likely hard to handle back in her prime. When I was younger, I spent a little time one summer at her house as my mother would run off for days at a time leaving me behind without anyone to take care of me.

That summer, she was gone for months.

I'm not sure who told Mrs. Gibson what was going on or how she even noticed.

She just showed up on the doorstep one day when I was around thirteen years old holding a plate piled high with the best tasting pork chops I'd ever eaten.

It became a routine. Several days would pass and she'd show up again.

Eventually she just flat out told me to be at her house at a very specific time for supper. It took a little while but eventually I showed up as she told me to.

My mom eventually showed back up one day just a few days before school started with clearer eyes, a more steady gait and words of apology.

I found out much later that she had run off to California that summer to party. She got so messed up one night not long after arriving that she passed out in an alley and was found by a good Samaritan who called an ambulance.

That good Samaritan cared enough to not only do that, but stay with her at the hospital and talk to her.

For some reason, my mom listened and took to heart everything that was said. She agreed to go to rehab and get her life straight.

It was while in rehab that she remembered she left me behind without a word to anyone.

I loved my mom, even at her worst. Forgiving her was easy, especially when she showed no signs of going back to that life.

She even moved us to a new house in a better part of town so that she wouldn't be tempted by those who sold her the drugs she was hooked on for so long.

Life for me was finally amazing. At least for a while.

She found out just a year later that she had hepatitis and it was shutting down her liver. She passed away slowly by the time I turned eighteen.

She's buried in a cemetery not too far out of town, surrounded by the flowers she loved so much.

Every Spring when the buttercups emerge in the fields around here, I go sit by her grave and enjoy the day.

Getting to my truck, I stuff the invoice for the parts I ordered in the glove box and start the truck up.

Picking up my phone, I dial my Prez to see if there's a reason any of our guys would be out by the old factory.

Being the Vice President, most everything goes through me first but I don't remember our guys needing to be out that way.

"Sup?" He answers.

"Were any of our guys out by the old factory?" I ask.

"Not that I know of. Why?"

"I ran into Mrs. Gibson and she said some guys on bikes almost ran her over. She thought they were part of the club because of the bikes but says she didn't recognize any of them."

"You on your bike or in a cage?" He asks.

"Cage."

"Ride by and see if you can spot anything then come back here. Fuck!" He growls, sounding worried.

"See ya in thirty." I say, putting the truck in drive.

"Be careful Grease."

"You know I will." I growl, annoyed.

"I'm still gonna say it brother. We almost lost you down South. I'm not fucking ready to watch another brother be put in the ground. See ya soon." He says quickly hanging up.

I know my club brothers care about me. After I lost my mom, this club is what saved me from the very path that she took. I'll always be grateful for that.

It doesn't take long to drive the short distance to the factory.

Going slowly but not slow enough to draw attention, I'm almost completely past it before I see any movement back behind one of the buildings.

I drive down to the next road and turn down it knowing it circles back behind it on the other side of the tree line.

Seeing a spot to pull over near a bridge where some older men are fishing, I shut the engine off and grab a fishing pole from the toolbox in the back.

I might as well make it look like I'm here for something other than to spy on the back of the factory.

"Fish biting?" I ask the men as I make my way to the bank.

"Not yet but Jimbo there seems to think he's gonna get a bigun." One man grunts before spitting his snuff on the ground.

I've never understood how the older generation can stomach the stuff. Straight powder from a can that stinks worse than anything you've ever smelled.

Making my way further along the bank, I'm farther into the trees and can no longer see the two men. Sitting my pole down, I walk into the woods several yards before the fence to the factory comes into view.

Staying hidden behind a tree, I kneel down and watch the doors out back. I don't have to wait long before I see several men walk outside.

They're too far away to hear what's being said but my eyes stay trained on the cuts they are wearing.

When they turn their back to me, heading back inside, I recognize the emblem on the back as that of the Demon Riders.

"Mother Fucker!" I whisper.

Moving further away carefully so I'm not seen, I make my way back to my pole, picking it up and heading back to my truck.

"That was fast." The man says as I pass by them once again.

"Wife called saying she needed something from the store." I shrug.

"Damn women always fuck up a man's day." The second man grumbles.

Getting to my truck, I throw the pole in the back and take off towards the clubhouse.

Reaper needs to know those fuckers are in the area and knowing they are here is bringing up questions of my own.

Britni

I'm standing in the kitchen when I hear Ja'sin come through the front door.

"Hey. Sorry I'm later than usual." He says, walking into the kitchen.

Looking at him, he's not smiling and his face looks worried.

"Everything okay at work?" I ask with concern.

"Hm? Oh, yeah, everything is fine."

"You look upset about something." I comment, turning back to the stove to turn off the oven and take the cornbread out.

"It's nothing we can't handle. What's for supper? It smells amazing." He changes the subject and I decide to drop it.

As we eat, he keeps up with conversation about everything except whatever was on his mind when he got home.

Remembering back to when I was still in the hospital about all the secret phone calls he was always making, I guess I shouldn't let the fact he doesn't talk to me about everything bother me. For some reason it does though.

When we head to bed, I go to the bathroom first, washing my face and brushing my teeth. Looking at myself in the mirror, I wonder if he truly feels anything for me at all.

I've noticed we never say I love you to each other. Shouldn't that be a very common phrase with a happily married couple?

I've tried more than once to get his attention physically. Maybe he's just not as attracted to me as I am to him.

With a sign, I walk out, turning the light off as I go. Ja'sin is already on his side of the bed waiting for me and I once again feel my nipples tingle with want.

Dreaming of him every night is taking a toll on me. There's a fire deep inside that I know only he can extinguish.

"Everything okay?" He asks when I stand there staring for too long.

"Why do you not want me?" I blurt out, surprising us both but I wait for him to answer anyway.

"Not want you? Why the hell would you think that?" He asks, sitting up on the side of the bed.

"Other than a few kisses, you've not touched me at all. What else am I supposed to think?" I demand but the grin on his face deepens.

"Come here." He commands and my feet move without thought until I'm standing in front of him. "You really think I don't want you?" He whispers, placing his hands on my sides, pushing my shirt up until he's touching my skin.

Chill bumps spread across my arms at his touch and I continue, staring into his eyes.

Eyes that are now completely focused on the skin exposed to his eyes as his hands continue to push my shirt up until he pulls it over my head.

"Fucking beautiful." He whispers, staring at my exposed breasts.

My nipples stand at attention, becoming hard nubs and poking out. He looks up into my eyes and slowly leans forward until his lips suck one into his mouth.

I throw my head back in ecstasy, grabbing his head to hold him close as he sucks harder. My core throbs with each pull of my nipple and he doesn't stop until I moan deep in my throat.

His arms come around my entire body as he lifts me up and lays me down on the bed. I didn't even realize he pulled my shorts off until he stands up, pulling them from my legs.

I'm unable to say a word as I watch him push his own shorts off, his hard cock springing out in front of him.

My mouth waters with the sight and I wonder if I will get a chance to feel it in my mouth.

Pushing my legs wide, he lays down between them until I feel his facial hair on my thighs. My lit throbs and I feel myself getting slicker, ready for whatever he does next.

"Not want you? Such crazy talk." I can feel his breath on my clit as he talks.

My heart races, my breathing is so fast I wonder if I'll hyperventilate but my eyes stay glued to his head, waiting for that first contact.

He doesn't take his time, instead he quickly dives deep with his tongue.

"Oh..." I groan and I feel him chuckle.

He fucks me with his tongue several times before moving to my clit, his tongue strumming it quickly.

I'm so close to an orgasm, I can't stop from bucking my hips against him but he pulls back before I fall over that edge.

I open my mouth to protest but he's over me quickly, slamming into me in one full thrust. It's all I need as I scream out my release.

He doesn't take long until he screams out his own. I hold his body to mine with my legs, his head laying on my chest and the only sound in the room is our fast breathing.

Guess I was wrong about him not wanting me. I think to myself with a chuckle. He looks up at me with a question in his eyes.

"Guess I was wrong." I say.

"Guess so." He answers as I feel his cock jump inside of me, getting hard once again.

I can't stop a grin that spreads across my face as I look into his eyes.

"We have some making up to do." He says, leaning up to kiss my neck and moving once again.

"I'm okay with that." I whisper back, enjoying all the sensations coursing through my body.

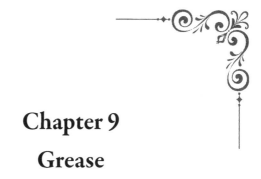

Chapter 9

Grease

"How do we know she isn't one of their spies?" Spark asks and I immediately feel my blood begin to boil.

"Why the fuck would you even ask such a thing?" I say through gritted teeth.

"He has a point, Grease. Several of us noticed the Demon Riders staring at her at the rally." Loki drawls from his seat across the table.

This is not how I expected Church to go with all my brothers. They're all putting the blame of these fucks being in our territory on Britni and the only thing I've seen her do is almost lose her life while on the back of my bike.

"Everyone just settle down. Britni is not a spy. I've already had Buzz from our sister chapter down South look into her background." Prez says with authority but there's something he's not told us yet judging by the look on his face.

"What did he find out?" I ask, genuinely curious about her past myself as we never got a chance to talk about everything before she lost her memory.

"To tell you the truth, not a whole hell of a lot before a few years ago. It's as if she just popped up one day."

"Sounds like spy shit to me." Loki laughs until I hit the table with my fist.

"Buzz thinks it's something else. He's looking deeper into it. He ran into what he called a roadblock in the servers. Whatever the fuck that means, I can't understand half the shit he spouts off. Until I hear back from either him or Skeeter, I want one of us on watch out at that factory at all times. I want to know their every fucking move. Got it?" He looks around the room at us all until everyone agrees.

"One more thing before this meeting is over..." He says and everyone stops getting up from their chairs.

"Not a fucking one of you are to treat that woman any differently than you did the day of the welcome home party. I will not stand for any of you mistreating a friend of this club." His eyes connect with all the brothers one at a time letting them know he means retribution if not obeyed.

I wait for everyone else to file out of the room before I get up from my seat.

"Don't be hard on them. They don't know her like you do." Prez says to me from the door.

"But that's just it, I don't really know her, do I? We were barely getting started before the accident." I rub my eyes trying to relieve the headache that is getting started.

"Brother, do you really believe the woman you see at home every single day is all that different from the one she was before bumping her head?" He asks but doesn't stay for an answer as he walks back down the hall.

He's right though. I don't think she's a different person just because she can't remember. Who we are is something that can't actually change. It's in us always.

Buzz not being able to find out anything about her from more than a few years back worries me though. Is Britni even her real name?

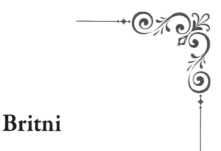

Britni

It's chasing me in the darkness. I can feel it breathing on me, ready to pounce at any second. I've got to get away but there's nowhere to hide.

As I turn the corner, it comes out of nowhere, snarling, grabbing me by the neck.

My eyes open on a scream as I thrash around on the bed.

"Britni! It's okay. It's just me." I feel someone shaking me and I look up into Ja'sin's eyes. "It's just me." He says once again and I stop moving.

"Ja'sin..." I throw myself into his arms as I begin to cry.

"Are you okay? That was some dream you were having."

"It was a nightmare." I mumble into his chest.

"Want to talk about it?" He asks but I shake my head no, burying my face further into his neck.

I finally notice that he's completely dressed and pull back to look at him.

"What time is it?" I ask.

"Around six. I was coming in to kiss you goodbye when I heard you screaming. You sure you're alright? I can get someone else to cover for me for a while longer if you need me to."

Shaking my head, I answer, "No. I'm fine really. Was just a silly dream that didn't mean anything."

"Why don't you come to work with me today? You can hang out around the shop, hand me the tools I need. Jade will probably be around too so you won't be the only woman there."

"Really? I can come with you?" I smile, bouncing on the bed until I'm on my feet next to it. "Give me ten minutes and I'll be ready to go!" I race off to the bathroom to get dressed with him laughing behind me.

"If I'd known that's all it took to make you this happy, I'd have suggested it last week." He says loud enough for me to hear.

Several hours later, I'm sitting with Jade in a chair behind the shop that's next door to the clubhouse, drinking lemonade when we hear a commotion over at the clubhouse.

All the men in the shop take off running in that direction.

"What's going on?" I ask, Jade and I both getting out of our chairs.

"It's not good. Come on, whatever it is, they may need our help." Jade takes off and I follow quickly behind her.

Whatever I was expecting it wasn't what my eyes found when we walked into the main room. All the guys are huddled around another man who is laying on a table with blood oozing from a wound in his arm.

There seems to be a buzzing sound in my head. The voices all around me fade into the background as my eyes scan the man on the table with a hole in his arm. A hole from a gunshot.

"Move!" I demand, coming closer. "Jade?" I look behind me for her. "Get me some boiling water, clean towels, some alcohol and find a pair of tweezers. Or pliers. Those will work too. Oh, and a sewing needle and strong thread." Jade stares at me with wide eyes before looking over at her husband who nods his head.

As she rushes off to get me what I need, I elbow my way closer and realize once I'm there that the man bleeding is Chains.

When I met him at the party, he seemed very intimidating but right now he looked more like he was about to pass out.

"You okay there, Chains?" I ask gently.

"Never better sweetheart." His reply makes me giggle.

"Stop flirting with my wife, Chains." I hear growled behind me, not having realized that Grease was right behind me.

"Grease, can you guys help get his shirt off please?" I ask with a grateful smile.

Several minutes later, Jade brings the supplies I asked for and my patient is laid back as comfortable as he is able to get.

"Okay, this is going to hurt." I look up into Chains' eyes.

"I won't move. Let's get this over with." He grunts but I notice that several of the men step closer before I start to dig into his arm.

I move the tweezers into his skin as gently as I can but he squirms a little.

A flash behind my eyes shoots an image across my brain of doing this very thing and a man hitting me in the temple. I squeeze my eyes closed tight.

"Britni? You okay?" I finally hear through the fog and open my eyes to see everyone staring at me with concern.

"I'm fine." I whisper and go back to digging for the bullet.

As I work, more images come at me. Faster and faster until I'm breathing rapidly but I don't stop working.

"You're turning white as a sheet. Someone else can do this." Grease says.

"No. I've got it. See?" I pull the tweezers from Chains' skin with the bullet pinched on the ends.

Throwing it onto the table, I clean up the skin on the arm with alcohol and then work on sewing it up.

"There. Good a s new." I say, exhaustion in my voice.

"Thank you, Nurse." Chains says with a smile.

Him calling me nurse sounds vaguely familiar.

"You're welcome." I smile back.

"Yes. Thank you Britni. We appreciate this more than you know." Reaper smiles. "Grease, you should take her home. She looks tired." He gives my husband a look I can't decipher but I'm too tired to try to understand.

Grease

B ritni fell asleep on the ride home and I carried her inside to our bed.

While she's been sleeping, I've been sitting on the couch watching the news to make sure no one reported gunshots in that part of town.

Of course they haven't. Most people around here are country folks and don't freak out over hearing a gunshot in the middle of summer when snakes are out in full force.

"How long did I sleep?" I hear from behind me and turn to see Britni shuffling into the room.

"About an hour or so. You okay?" I ask as she sits on the couch next to me.

"Yeah. I just got worn out I guess." She rubs her eyes with her hand. "Am I a nurse?" She blurts out and I turn to look at her.

"Yeah. A damn good one too." I answer truthfully.

She shakes her head, turning to stare at the T.V.

"You clearly remembered what to do. What else do you remember?" I ask slowly.

"I'm not sure yet. It's all a jumble. Up here. Ya know?" She rubs her temples.

"At least it's all trying to come back though right?" I smile although I don't really feel like smiling.

If she remembers, when she does, will she leave? I've gotten used to having her here and referring to her as my wife has become second nature.

"I guess it's a good thing." She shrugs.

"You guess? I figured you'd want all your memories back."

"I did. At first anyway. But I'm no longer sure they're good memories." She whispers, looking sad.

Raising up, I turn her face to mine. "We have good memories."

Her smile brightens. "Yes. We certainly do and I'm sure the ones I still don't remember were good too."

Pulling her close to me, I close my eyes and breath in her scent. I truly hope that our memories together, all of them, are greater than whatever is in her past.

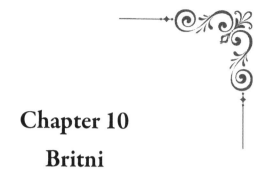

Chapter 10
Britni

For the last several days, I've remembered quite a lot from before my accident although I've not shared everything with Grease.

I feel bad for keeping quiet about knowing that we aren't really married but I don't want to leave. I'm afraid that if he knows then what we currently have will be over.

I'm pretty damn certain that I'm in love with the man but what if he doesn't feel the same way?

I need someone that I can talk to about it which is why I called Jade earlier to see if she would stop by for a while.

When I hear knocking at the door, I know that it's here so I swing it open with a smile.

"You called so here I am." She passes me a hot cup of coffee she must have picked up at the gas station on her way over.

"Thank you but I could have made us a pot in the kitchen."

"Not this, you couldn't. Give it a try and you'll see what I mean." She nods at the cup in my hand as we walk into the kitchen.

Lifting the cup, I gingerly take a sip as it's really hot. The taste of chocolate hits my taste buds first but it's the zing hidden just underneath the chocolate that catches my attention.

"What is that?" I ask, opening the lid to look inside but all I see is what appears to be coffee with creamer.

"A very special family recipe." She wags her brows.

"Alcohol. You put alcohol in the coffee?" I laugh.

"Hell yeah. Just a little. Not enough to do anything but isn't it delish? My sister actually got me attached to this shit and as long as it's in a "to go" cup, no one will ever know."

"Your sister is a bad influence. A fun one but bad just the same."

"Being bad is always fun." I hear a voice behind me and I jump almost spilling my cup.

"Fire. I didn't hear you come in." I hold my hand over my heart where it's jumping in my chest.

"I noticed." She says dryly, walking over to the table and taking a seat.

"I'm sorry. I wasn't meaning what I said to sound like a bad thing." I apologize.

"No worries. At least you think I'm fun. My brother in law thinks I'm mental."

I'm not quite sure what to say to that when both Fire and Jade start laughing. It's so infectious, I start laughing too.

"I heard about you setting fire to a cabin he was sleeping in." At my mention of the cabin, she laughs yet again.

"That night is forever burned in my memory." She chuckles and her sister just shakes her head.

"You could have killed him." Jade says.

"I was trying to but the fucker woke up, ran outside in his birthday suit, stumbling around until his naked ass fell in the rose bushes. And that's where the other guys found him. Thorns stuck to his ass and balls. Was awesome!"

"Jesus. I thought Grease was making up most of it."

"Nope. Grease would never lie." Jade shakes her head and Fire agrees.

"He's been lying about us being married though." I pop off and both women swing their heads to stare at me.

"You remember?" Fire asks.

"Yes and no. There's still some stuff that's kind of fuzzy but I do remember that I am definitely not married. And that is why I called you over here." I look at Jade.

"I don't follow." Her brows draw together.

"She's afraid if she tells Grease she remembers that part then he may want her to leave. Is that not right?" Fire says with a grin.

"That's it exactly." I sigh, plopping down into a chair.

Both women go quiet for several long minutes and I think they aren't going to say anything.

"I think you should tell him. If he wants you to leave then he's not the man for you." Jade says and I look up from the table. "From what we've seen," she points between her and her sister, "that's not what is going to happen."

"You don't think so?" I ask as hope floods my heart.

"No. We don't think so. He looks at you in a way that only a man in love looks at a woman." Fire says with a faraway look that I don't understand.

"Now. Tell us what you remember." Jade changes the subject drawing the attention from her sister's sad look.

Grease

"We have news from Buzz on Britni." Prez says, looking around the room until he stops on me waiting for me to deliver what news I have.

"She's also started remembering some stuff. Just bits and pieces." I tell the guys.

"Go ahead and tell them what you know and I think with that, what Buzz has sent us can fill in the rest." Prez says and I sigh, not liking a damn bit of it.

"It started with a nightmare she had the morning Chains caught a bullet. It was of a hyena chasing her." I watch as all the brothers' lean closer with interest. "She didn't tell me about it until a few days ago when she started to actually get flashes of memories that were giving her migraines."

"What else has she remembered, brother?" Bud asks in the quiet room when I stare off into the distance for too long.

"She had a flash about being taken from the hospital where she was working. They must have had her for quite a while. She remembers being made to nurse the men. Bullet wounds, cuts, scrapes, knife wounds, whatever they needed." I trail off once again.

"If they had her for a while, does that mean they used her as well?" Aero almost whispers across the room but we all know it's not a good sign when his voice gets that low.

All I can do is look up at my brother. I don't have it in me to voice what I've learned in only a few short days. If I ever do the anger inside of me is likely to destroy this entire fucking town.

"So how did she get away?" Loki asks.

"Britni currently doesn't remember that part so this is where the Intel from Buzz comes in." Prez speaks up and I slump further into my chair, thankful I don't have to keep talking about the other shit.

I drown out the voices around me having already read everything sent to us from Buzz. My girl's name really is Britni at least her middle name is.

I can't believe the fucking FBI has left her all alone, in the fucking wind as they continue an investigation instead of locking up the mother fuckers who not only kidnapped then imprisoned an innocent woman but used her against her will.

And they seriously wonder why we hate them so fucking much.

"So when are we planning to burn that fucking factory to the ground with them assholes inside?" Hammer's question pulls me back to the conversation at hand.

"As soon as Grease comes up with a plan." My eyes jump to him with his answer. "This is your woman so I think it's only right you get to put all this together. Whatever you want, brother. We're behind you all the fucking way."

All my brothers bang their fists on the table at the same time. It's a tradition to show that we are all in agreement.

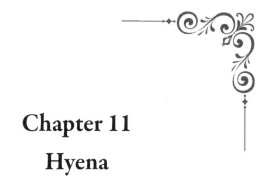

Chapter 11
Hyena

"We've been here for weeks and haven't seen her." Beeks argues and I'm tempted to put a bullet in his head my fucking self.

"She's here damn you! I want you mother fuckers outside every fucking grocery store in this god forsaken town until you see her! She's gotta eat, right? We know she left that fucking hospital with the Night Howler's. They were crawling all over the place which is why we couldn't get to her down south but I am not leaving here without her!" I scream at the men in front of me.

I watch them all as they file out of the room, waiting for just one to say something so I have an excuse to cut their asses down but no one says a word.

"Mother fuckers." I growl to the now empty room.

That bitch is here somewhere. She knows we saw her down south. I'm surprised really she wasn't able to give a better description of the one who ran her down but for once, one of those fuckers did something right.

It was a big surprise to find out she was at the rally and in the company of another club. A bitch ass club at that. They went soft when the last President of the club died and his son took over.

How the fuck can you make a living going legit any fucking way? I curl my lip at the thought. I love money too fucking much for that. Which is why I need that stupid bitch back.

When I had her around, my club didn't need to go to the hospital where they ask too many fucking questions. Being able to fuck that bitch whenever I wanted and however I wanted was a fucking bonus.

I can feel my cock getting hard just thinking about all the squirming and screaming she did while under me. That's how I know she loved it no matter how much she pretended otherwise.

No one else was allowed to touch her. She was all mine. Basically my ol' lady without the official title. What more could a woman want?

Adjusting myself, I grab my cigarettes and head outside to double check that those bastards did what I fucking told them to do.

Pretty soon I'll have my woman back where she belongs and I'll make certain she never leaves again.

Britni

I pace the floor in the kitchen as I wait for Jade to get here. I called her earlier when I realized that I've not had a monthly period for as long as, well I don't exactly know since I can't remember everything just yet.

From what Jade told me, I met Grease at her wedding which was two months ago now and I have an entry on a calendar I found in one of my bags that was with me at the rally that shows I was on my period the week before that.

But I have no memory of one since. The only thing that made me think about it was when I felt sick this morning after eating breakfast.

None of it stayed down and I wasn't running a fever. I don't even feel bad like I would if I were getting sick.

I called Jade asking her to go get me a test as I'm currently not allowed to leave the house without an escort and there's a prospect watching the house from outside to be sure I stay put.

Well, he's there to make sure no one comes in too but I'm starting to feel like a prisoner.

Banging on the door makes me jump but I rush to answer it knowing it has to be Jade.

"Hurry." I rush her inside, shutting the door behind her. "Did anyone see you?" I ask, looking out the window.

"Of course they saw me coming." Jade giggles as I slit my eyes at her.

"That's not what I meant."

"No one saw me buying this." She rolls her eyes, handing me a small paper sack that I take from her and clutch to my chest.

"Jesus." I whisper, closing my eyes while holding that tiny bag.

"Well go take it!" Jade demands, pushing me towards the hall. "I'll be in the kitchen."

As I walk into the bathroom, I feel as if I am doomed.

"Why does everything have to happen to me?" I ask, looking up at the ceiling.

Taking the text out of the package, I hold it in my hand until I'm sitting on the toilet.

"Here goes nothing." I say as I begin to pee on the stick.

Once I'm finished, I set it on the counter, looking away from it while I finish cleaning myself and pulling my shorts back up.

I take my time flushing the toilet and washing my hands, trying to slow my racing heart but it just keeps beating erratically in my chest.

Thinking that I've waited long enough, I lean over the test and look at it.

The smiling face that's looking back at me makes me wonder if the makers designed it as a mocking type gesture because I am not smiling back currently.

"What the fuck am I going to do?" I whisper in the quietness of the bathroom, not expecting an answer. One comes through the door anyway, making me laugh.

"You're going to get off the door so I can come in and see too!" Jade says loudly.

Opening the door, she looks at my face then at the test on the counter, turning to me with a wide grin.

"Awe, you're going to have a mini Grease." She says and I burst into tears.

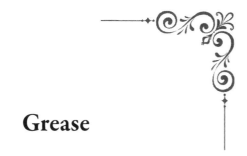

Grease

I look around the room at the men ready to stand with me in the battle ahead. All of my club brothers are here as well as a few friends from out of state.

Baratta and Gio are two brothers we've had business with before through our sister chapter down in Nola as well as through the Wolfsbane MC whose Prez is the brother in law to Reaper.

They're twins from the Marcus mob family who also work in the private sector. Basically they are snipers for hire and the government uses them both to their full advantage all around the world.

They're fingerprints are untraceable and there's no paper trail to even say they exist. They're ghosts which is what the two brothers are known as.

They brought along another guy that was introduced to me as Jay. He has the same serious look as the other two with eyes that clearly tell a tale of all the death he's seen.

"So what's the plan?"

"The Carter boys will cause a distraction on the farthest end of town from the factory to keep the city cops busy. Hopefully nothing that will land them in juvenile hall." I look to see if Bones is going to protest since he's basically adopted the boys. "County Mounties will be called out further into the county."

"This will distract them all?" Jay asks with raised brows.

"We only have two of each on duty at any given moment. Our town is fairly small." I shrug.

"What about Full-Growns?" Bud asks while the guys not from our club look confused.

"Full-Growns is what we call Highway Patrol." I explain to them. "I called in some favors with all the loggers we know. We may owe a few for maintenance on their trailers." I look at Reaper who nods in agreement.

Most of our business comes from building and maintaining log trailers for all the logging crews. Around here it's a big business with a lot of money to be made.

"The plan is for all of you to cause a ruckus to draw them all out. Reaper, Gio, Jay, Baratta and myself will be scattered along the back perimeter at the fence line to take them out one by one.

There's just one exception...I want Hyena, their President, alive. At least long enough for me to be close enough to watch his life fade." I growl.

"What about the bodies? I'm assuming I will blow some shit up today." Aero asks excitedly.

"Yes, you get to blow up some shit." We all laugh. "But the bodies won't be included. I need Chucky to be close by with one of his trucks and enclosed trailers for us to load all the bodies into.

They'll all have bullets in them so we can't leave them at the scene. Blowing the place up will get rid of the other evidence."

Everyone shakes their heads in agreement.

"I need everyone to have their head in the game. I won't be putting any brothers in an unmarked grave today. Understood?" Prez asks and waits for everyone to agree.

"The time window on this will still be short even with all the distractions we have in place for all the cops.

As soon as Grease gives the green light, everyone moves in and we get out as quickly as possible with no one the wiser.

Be sure to take the back-roads getting back here. All this preparation would be for nothing if everyone in town sees us coming or going."

"Let's go kiss our women boys and be ready to head out by nine tonight." I say and everyone gets up to leave the room.

"This should be fun practice. Why such a long ass face, Jay." Gio asks his friend as they walk out of the room.

"Your friend okay?" I ask Baratta as we are the last out the door.

"He'll be fine. It's just woman troubles as always." He chuckles walking away.

"I can relate." I whisper into the now empty hall.

Britni

"What do you mean I have to stay at the clubhouse? Just where are you going so late at night?" I demand, one hand on my hip.

The look he's currently giving me clearly says he expected me to just blindly follow without any questions. I've finally realized that not asking questions just isn't me.

Besides, knowing now that there's a possible baby on the way, it's better that I learn a whole lot more about the man that my heart now belongs to. Will he be pissed that I didn't tell him as soon as I found out?

"What has gotten into you?" He asks with concern.

"What do you mean?"

"You seem. I don't know. Just different today. Are you okay? Are the headaches getting worse? I can take you to the doctor tomorrow and get you checked out."

"No. I'm fine. Really." I smile brightly. "Just tell me why I need to stay at the clubhouse tonight. Please. I've more than noticed that you hide things from me and I've tried to not let it bother me but the truth is that it does."

"I know we've not had a lot of time to talk about the rules of an MC since your accident but the short answer is there will always be some things that I can't share with you. It's more to protect you and protect the club than anything else."

He looks so earnest in his explanation that I realize I believe and trust him completely. But it also brings up more questions in my mind. Is what he's doing illegal?

Thinking about all the guys in the club that I've gotten to know recently, I can't see any of them doing anything illegal that would be hurtful to another unless it was in trying to protect the club.

"Fine. I'll go to the clubhouse but what we can share with each other is still up for debate at a later date." I raise one brow before turning and walking away.

I'm only two steps away when I hear him laughing hard. Instead of acknowledging the laughter, I keep walking. He'll find out soon enough I'm not a pushover.

Grease

Looking at the piles of bodies as I pass by, I check each face for the fucker that hurt my girl but none of them are him.

"Anyone seen Hyena?" I yell to all my guys as they busily try to get the bodies loaded into the trailer.

"I think this is your guy." I turn to find Jay dragging a man with his feet and hands tied together.

He drops him in front of me giving him a sharp kick to the ribs.

"I found him hiding under a desk. He's a very bad shot by the way. He ran out of bullets." Jay grins, kicking Hyena once again and watching him struggle to breath. "Oh, he does have a few holes in his lungs. Both of which have probably collapsed by now so you may want to do whatever it is you were planning quickly."

Jay walks away whistling a jaunty tune with a better attitude than he had earlier today. He's just like the twins, Baratta and Gio, killing puts a mighty pep to their step as well.

Kneeling down to the asshole at my feet, I can see that his lips are turning blue from the lack of oxygen to his lungs. It's one hell of a way to die and I wish I had thought of it.

His eyes look at me wildly, almost begging for me to release him from the pain and suffering but I just smile.

"This is a hell of your own making. You deserve much worse and I hope your ass hangs on until my brothers fill the hole they will throw you in with dirt."

I continue watching him struggle, blood oozing from his mouth.

"We have the rest, Grease. We need to go." Chucky says from beside me.

Hyena's body starts shaking, his chest trying to rise one last time until he stops moving completely. His eyes glaze over, looking empty of life.

"Take him." I nod and several of the guys step in to grab the body, throwing it into the trailer and shutting the door.

"I'm all set. Let's go!" Aero races out of the factory.

We can hear sirens in the distance, still far enough away for the blast to not hurt anyone.

Hopping onto the back of the nearest back with one of my brothers, we all take off down the road. We're about a mile away when the blast lights up the skies.

We may have destroyed a building but it was already slated for demolition in a couple of months. We just made it happen a little sooner is all.

Knowing that my woman is now safe lifts some of the weight I've felt on my shoulders since our accident. There's still another weight there though. One that is afraid that she won't want to stay with me.

Rubbing my hand over the middle of my chest, I hope that won't be the case.

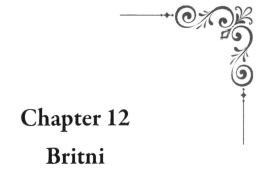

Chapter 12
Britni

It's been a few days since the night I had to stay at the clubhouse with the other girls while all the men went somewhere.

They really weren't gone for very long, not all of them anyway and they all came back more than ready to eat.

Jade was pretty quiet until I kept pestering her and asking questions. What she had to tell me really opened my eyes about these men although I can't say that I am too surprised.

They aren't my first encounter with a motorcycle club even though they seem to be a better one than the one I was forced to be in for a while.

I've had a lot of time to think over everything and know that I need to set Grease down today for a much needed, overdue talk.

He should be home from work at any minute so I double check that the table is set for dinner.

I'm just carrying over the fried chicken I made, setting it in the middle of the table when I hear his boots coming through the door.

"Something smells great!" He sniffs the air, walking into the kitchen with a smile.

"We have fried chicken, homemade coleslaw, baked beans and mashed potatoes with gravy." I grin at his face as he surveys the table.

"Jesus woman, there's enough here to feed an army." He laughs.

"Then I guess we'll have left overs tomorrow." I state as my stomach growls loudly.

I've been unable to eat earlier in the day because of morning sickness but by the late afternoon, I'm starving and will eat almost everything my eyes land on.

"Let's eat before that stomach of yours eats your backbone." He grins at me when I slap his shoulder.

We talk about his day at work and the things I got up to today while we eat. We're just finishing up the last bite when I tell him, "We need to talk." His eyes catch mine, looking sad at first.

"I was afraid of this." He murmurs.

"Afraid of what?" I ask quickly.

"You remember everything now, don't you? You remember that we aren't really married." He says dejectedly.

"I remembered that two weeks ago." I shrug, his head spinning back to me.

"You didn't say anything." He states.

"I was afraid you'd make me leave."

"And now you want to leave?" He asks.

"No. I don't." I answer honestly.

"Oh, thank God." He grabs my hand, pulling it to his lips, kissing my wrist. "If you don't want to leave me then what's all this about?" He finally asks.

"I'm going to have a baby." I blurt out, pulling my hand away.

His face looks confused and then shocked.

"Um..." His eyes look around the room wildly and I wonder what he's thinking.

"You don't want it." It's now my turn to look sad.

"Hey, I didn't say that." He gets out of his chair, kneeling at my feet.

"The look on your face says that." I feel tears in my eyes.

"No, baby, that's not what's on my face. I'm just not sure what you are wanting me to say. Women these days hold all the cards. Do you want to keep it? Because if you don't, I'll still stand behind your choice even if I don't like it." He sighs.

"Seriously? You'd let me do that?" I raise my brows.

"I wouldn't like it one damn bit, just so you know but it's your body. Only you can decide what to do with it."

I stare at him truly surprised at the wonder this man actually is. There's not many like him. Hell there's none like him and he's completely mine.

Smiling back at his face as the tears leave my eyes, I say, "I sure do love you."

"I sure do love you too." He says with a grin of his own before pulling me in for a kiss.

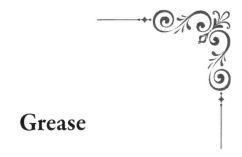

Grease

Life with Britni has been amazing the last several months. We have an appointment today to see what the baby is going to be.

She thinks I want a boy but I actually would love a little girl. Girls are easier I think to keep alive than boys and I told her so.

She laughed so hard at me about it that she almost peed all over herself that night.

I meant it though. Boys are rough, always looking for the next thing to get into.

Take the Carter boys for example. Just the other day they got into the shed that holds all of Aero's stuff and nearly blew up the entire clubhouse.

So, a sweet little sassy girl would suit me just fine. I'm too old for what a boy would get into. He'd probably put me into an early grave.

"You heading to the appointment?" Prez asks as I make my way to the door.

"Yeah. Britni is supposed to meet me there. She was going to the mall with Jade for a while first."

"Yes. I heard about that this morning as Jade grabbed my wallet for my credit card." He rolls his eyes. "Apparently Cole needs new ball shoes and Amber needs a dress for the pageant at the school."

"Sounds like you'll be lucky to have anything left on your card then. Those dresses are expensive." Joanna laughs from the office door. "You let us know as soon as you are done at the doctor's office, Grease. We need to know what we're buying for the newest tiny member." She smiles, going back to the desk to answer the phone.

"Let's us know, brother." Prez waves me off as I leave.

An hour later, I'm in a tiny room with Britni laying on a bed, her belly uncovered. The technician puts some kind of gel on her and starts moving this tiny device around.

Within seconds we hear a tiny heart beat and it still makes my own jump no matter how many times I hear it.

She starts taking measurements and pointing out things as she goes. I'm almost jumping from one foot to the next waiting for her to get on with it.

"Let's see what we have here." Her hands move slightly and I try to make out what's on the screen but I can't make out a damn thing. "Do you guys want to know the sex?"

"Yes." I answer quickly and Britni laughs.

"Excuse him please. He's a little excited." Britni, pats my hand with a grin.

"That's alright. It's great when the fathers are so involved. It looks like you are having a sweet baby girl." I smile broadly at the technician.

"Thank, God!" I whisper, unable to look anywhere but at the screen.

"You just made his day." I hear Britni say. "He thinks boys are harder." They both start laughing at that.

"Boy is he gonna be surprised." The technician says.

I'm having a girl. A beautiful baby girl. With the absolute love of my life.

My life is fucking awesome!

The End....For Now...

Available Now!
Fang's Miracle
Wolfsbane Ridge MC Book 7

Fuck Cancer.

And fuck the sperm donor that decided we weren't worth the trouble—the day we received our baby girl's results.

The doctors in Alaska were great, but Olivia needed more. Forced to pack-up our entire world, alone, I searched for an expert willing to operate. When we finally found him, the real trouble began...

How would we ever find a donor in time?

Olivia's life was on the line; our days together were running out. When a leather covered biker walked through the door, I never expected him to be our miracle. My miracle.

Turns out, we needed a lot more saving than I realized.

https://books2read.com/FangsMiracle

Coming November 14, 2023

Snake's Fate

Wolfsbane Ridge MC Book 8

Snake

Computers and Harley's are forever. Women are for one night. That's how I've lived my life for the past nine years, never letting anyone in.

My life has been amazing inside the Wolfsbane MC. These men are more than friends, they are my brothers. Everything in life was going great...until she showed up again with bad news and a secret that rocks me to my core.

Andi

I knew it would be hard for him to find out this way. He disappeared from town almost ten years ago without even a note, I wasn't expecting to run into him again after all these years.

His eyes are now filled with anger. I just don't know if it's directed at me or the circumstances that got us to this point.

I should have made different choices back then. We all should have.

https://books2read.com/SnakesFate

Coming July 7, 2023
Shelby's Secret
Poison Pen Book 6

D ivorced with two kids, Shelby Lynn Porter needs a place to hide from her ex-husband. When he tried to attack her in the courtroom she saw her life flash before her eyes.

Being the only child of celebrity parents puts her in the spotlight, which is the last place she wants to be.

Glitch loves his life. Partying it up with the local MC, women at his beck and call, riding the roads with nothing to hold him back. He has no plans to change that, until he sets his eyes on her.

Taylor and Arin's new nanny is one hot mama and he wants her, but is he ready for a family?

Is Shelby ready to move on from the trauma of her past and allow someone else in?

https://books2read.com/ShelbysSecret

Available NOW!

Giovanni's Obsession

G iovanni

Catching a man beating the life out of a woman in a back alley doesn't usually grab my attention. That is, unless that woman happens to be Raven. The waitress at the local diner. I don't usually frequent the same establishment more than once if I can help it. It's easier to stay hidden that way.

Feeling this odd pull towards her, I try to fight it. But seeing her broken unleashes the rage inside that only her touch seems to calm. I'll kill whoever did this, even if it kills me.

Raven

My life has never been my own. I ran away to a new city thinking I was small potatoes compared to everything else. I was wrong. HE wants me back. According to his thugs, he doesn't care in what condition I return either. This time though, I'm not alone. This handsome as sin man that looks more dangerous than those I've run from. But when I look into his eyes, I feel pulled to him. When his hands touch mine, a spark ignites that just might consume us both. Will new found love save them? Or will it strike a fatal blow?

https://books2read.com/GiovannisObsession

Connect with the Author

Website:
www.authormarissaann.com[1]

Facebook:
https://www.facebook.com/MarissaAnnAuthor

Instagram:
https://www.instagram.com/authormarissaann/

Twitter:
https://twitter.com/marissaannbooks

Goodreads:
https://www.goodreads.com/author/show/18159855.Marissa_Ann

Linkedin:
https://www.linkedin.com/in/marissa-ann-ballard-93982b186/

Tik Tok
https://www.tiktok.com/@authormarissaann

Bookbub:
https://www.bookbub.com/profile/marissa-ann

Other Titles by Marissa Ann

Book 1 Buzz
https://books2read.com/BuzzNewOrleans
Book 2 Skeeter
https://books2read.com/Skeeter
Giovanni's Obsession
https://books2read.com/GiovannisObsession
All I've Got
https://books2read.com/AllIveGot
Poison Pen Series
Book 1 Baratta's Darkness
https://books2read.com/BarattasDarkness
Book 2 Lily's Shadow
https://books2read.com/LilysShadow
Book 3 Arin's Light
https://books2read.com/ArinsLight
Book 4 Mika's Heart
https://books2read.com/MikasHeart
Book 5 Cass' Vow
https://books2read.com/CassVow
Book 6 Shelby's Secret
https://books2read.com/ShelbysSecret

Printed in Great Britain
by Amazon